PUFFIN BOOKS

KISS THE LINES

Coming from a defence background, Vinamra Srivastava has spent most of his life hopping across all corners of India. He graduated from the Indian Institute of Management, Ahmedabad, in 2008. Since then, he has been a management consultant based in Singapore.

An avid sportsman, keen debater and a fan of old Hindi songs, Vinamra now hopes that this book, his debut effort, is only the beginning of many more to come.

KISS THE LINES

VINAMRA SRIVASTAVA

PUFFIN BOOKS

An imprint of Penguin Random House

PUFFIN BOOKS

USA | Canada | UK | Ireland | Australia
New Zealand | India | South Africa | China | Singapore

Puffin Books is part of the Penguin Random House group of companies
whose addresses can be found at global.penguinrandomhouse.com

Published by Penguin Random House India Pvt. Ltd
4th Floor, Capital Tower 1, MG Road,
Gurugram 122 002, Haryana, India

Penguin
Random House
India

First published in Puffin by Penguin Books India 2013

10 9 8 7 6 5 4 3 2

ISBN 9780143331797

Typeset in Bembo Std by Eleven Arts, Keshav Puram, New Delhi
Printed at Repro India Limited

www.penguin.co.in

contents

Acknowledgements

My life would have been on a different path had some people not supported and guided me in this debut endeavour. I thank them from the depths of my heart:

Shruti, my better half—for all the weekends that you lost because of this book, for all the times you read and reread the drafts without complaining, and for all the sacrifices you made!

Vaishali, Jaya, Sohini and Amrita, my editors-in-charge, as well as my publisher Penguin, for not only showing faith in the book from the start, but also patiently guiding a first-time author through the nuances of fiction writing.

My first two reviewers even before I could find an editor, Swati Bhabhi and Indu Mummy, your insights made the book sharp enough. I promise you will get repeat jobs soon!

Mom, Dad, Bhaiya—I guess the writing habit that you inculcated in me from school days is starting to pay off!

Last, but not the least, Saina Nehwal, thank you so much for being my inspiration and for being kind enough to write a few lines for the book. May you continue to bring laurels to the country and inspire us all.

And now, as the chair umpire would say—'Play!'

Foreword

There is a lot of difference between fiction and real life. However, this book has managed to show what goes into the making of a badminton champion quite realistically. I myself had to work very hard at a tender age to get where I am today.

In order to succeed, one must never lose focus. I remember in December 2002 I had reached the finals of five events— the Under-13 singles and doubles, the Under-16 singles and doubles and the Under-19 singles. I lost only in the Under-16 singles, which, unfortunately was the criterion for selection to the junior team for the European tour. Although I won the other four titles, my coach was not happy. He told me that I should not have participated in so many events. What was the use, as I lost in the event that was the most crucial.

So, winning and losing is part of life in the game. I believe in staying positive and hope others will also follow this. At the same time, one should be focused, dedicated and fit. Keeping two goals in mind will not yield good results. I would say, choose one and keep the other as a hobby. If you are doing well in studies and want to stay in academics, sports are good to keep you focused and healthy. If you're good at sports and want to pursue that, then don't completely abandon your studies as they will keep you up to date.

Follow this principle and you'll always stay on track!

Saina Nehwal
18 May 2010

Prologue

'It's here!'

Kavya stormed into the house in her trademark state of excitement, the newspaper in her hand brushing against a little showpiece that had adorned our drawing room for ages.

Crash!

'Oops.' She looked at Mom sheepishly. 'I am so sorry, aunty.'

With a mischievous expression, Mom taunted, 'Oh, not at all, beta! Breaking stuff is your birthright and you shall have it.'

We all laughed.

Kavya gave her a quick hug. 'You are a darling, aunty.'

I must admit that Kavya's chirpy presence was one of the key reasons why my family had recovered from the shock much quicker. She would always have her own way in the house and no one could say a thing. In fact, everyone at home adored her craziness . . . it brought some cheer into our lives.

Kavya neatly laid out the newspaper on the centre table and started reading the main article on the sports page.

My eyes rested on the paper, but gradually, I felt Kavya's voice fading away. My mind started to journey back in time, and the past *five years that had turned my life upside down was now flashing in front of my eyes.*

It all seemed like yesterday . . . every moment still so vivid.

1

That fateful night

The decibel levels in the stadium had reached deafening proportions, and the energy in the air had engulfed everyone. I stood by the courtside gasping frantically for breath, and could barely hear my coach through the din.

'Push her back in the deep corners and engage her in long rallies. She's too strong for you at the net.' He had to shout, but maintained a calm tone. 'Build up the point patiently and wear her down, Payal. You have stretched her excellently in the first game. She's getting tired. Just capitalize on that now.'

My mind was racing. I still couldn't believe I had wasted a game point to hand Ritu the game 21–23 after running her so close. My hands were trembling and I was desperately trying to put the enormity of the situation out of my mind.

'Time,' the umpire announced.

I started the second game cautiously and slowly developed a good rhythm. The cheers in the stadium showed no signs of subsiding. I had to muster all my strength to play at the baseline, but Ritu showed no signs of tiredness. At 10–9, I shifted gears. I knew I had to take the lead before going into the mid-game break. There was a spring in my feet now; I started jumping high and smashing the shuttle hard. But Ritu was retrieving everything that came her way with great tenacity and technical prowess.

And then it came—the trademark that had been my saviour on the circuit thus far. I jumped and, with great power, hit a cross-court smash from behind my head. Ritu was not ready for this. She scampered, lunged and fell on the court . . . but could not reach the impeccably placed smash. I was ecstatic! I pumped my fists and let out a wild cry. My opponent was on the floor; I knew I was back in business.

As the stadium erupted, I threw a quick glance towards Bhaiya. The smile on his lips reassured me of his pride at my prowess despite the immense pressure. He cheered me on enthusiastically.

I tried my best to play only at the four corners of the court. My combination of drops and smashes was rewarded and, within no time, I had deflated my opponent and pocketed the second game 21–16.

The crowd was on its feet, applauding. Breathless and exhausted, I paced up and down the side of the court while my coach shouted animatedly, 'Hit more cross-court, Payal; she's just blocking your side smashes and making you run diagonal on the court to pick—that's why you lost control of some of the rallies.' He was moving both his hands in the air frantically and looking rather funny.

Despite my comeback, I was finding it tough to stay still and focus. My heartbeat was rising and my legs were tiring. I had never been comfortable with three-game matches; nervousness and fitness had always been my nemeses.

On the other side of the court, Ritu stood firm with her head down, looking at the court and listening patiently to her coach. Senior to me by three years, this situation was nothing new to her. She knew she had the experience to come back with a vengeance. She kept nodding as her coach drew his plans on paper. Quietly and confidently, the team was working out a strategy.

As we stepped on the court for the final time, a loud roar reverberated across the hall and screams of 'Come on, Ritu!' filled my ears.

I shook them off and got going aggressively, starting to smash very early in the rally. But this was not my natural game. I was tiring and wanted to end the points quickly.

Though leading 10–6, I was panting while Ritu kept her calm. It was her turn to dictate the points now, as her strategy started to unfold. Without trying anything fancy, she stuck to the basics and kept on pushing me towards the backhand back corner, shot after shot. And suddenly, without changing her action, she played a fine cross-court drop near the net! Taken by surprise, I had to cover the full diagonal of the court and my tired legs found it increasingly tough to respond.

Ritu's smart tactics and my failing fitness levels reduced the score to 19–19. There was palpable tension in the air. It had boiled down to a battle of nerves and stamina.

Ritu served high and long. My eyes followed the shuttle closely as my feet started stepping back. I stood at the edge of the baseline but was still indecisive whether the shuttle would go in or out. My hands trembled; fear clouded my mind and conflicting voices screamed inside my head. I took too long to judge and had to let the shuttle drop . . . I looked pleadingly at the line judge . . . there was a moment's silence . . . the crowd held its breath . . . my coach closed his eyes . . .

After some agonizing microseconds, the judge signalled that it was in! Ritu's camp erupted and I stood motionless. The pressure-cooker atmosphere was getting to me. I knew it was now or never.

'You have trained so hard, Payal! Have you forgotten those tiring sessions in the gym and the long hours on court? Come on, girl, you are so close, you can beat her . . .' I urged myself on loudly. Coach was vivaciously feeding me last-minute advice from the sidelines and I could see Bhaiya chewing his nails in anticipation.

I closed my eyes and let out a short sigh to calm myself. Down by a match point, it was the biggest test of my character. I decided that aggression would be my best defence. Ritu served short, but I had already rushed forward. I jumped high and smashed with all my might. Ritu dived and barely picked it up . . . the crowd was on its feet, screaming . . . I sensed blood . . . before Ritu could recover, I jumped high again and smashed hard cross-court. With lightning speed, the shuttle beat Ritu and landed right on the sideline—I had saved the match by finding the line just in time!

Once again I pumped my fist towards my coach and shouted. He gestured with both hands, telling me to keep my cool.

At 20–20, I'm sure Ritu's mind was racing as much as mine. I took an extra second to soothe my nerves. This was going to be the most critical serve of my career. I shivered; the service touched the net cord and I stared in dismay as it fell back on my side . . . after so much hard work to save the game, I had made an unforced error at the most crucial of times!

Ritu grinned at her luck as my desperate eyes searched for Bhaiya in the crowd. He tried his best to smile and nodded his head slightly to encourage me.

As Ritu served at 21–20, my mind went numb. I could see years of sweat, struggle and toil flash past my eyes. This was the Junior National Championships; there was too much at stake—my badminton career, my dreams, my future.

Ritu attacked incessantly while panic and fatigue threatened to overwhelm me. However, I kept defending valiantly as I searched for one more chance to draw level. But Ritu had her own plans. She jumped high to prepare for the kill. I moved further back to defend. She reached the shuttle in mid-air but instead of punching it, deceptively touched it, letting it drop right near the net. Taken aback, I stopped my retreat and jumped forward desperately. I fell on the court, missed the shuttle by a whisker and prayed for it to go out. As I lay on the court watching the white feathers glide by, I felt my destiny slipping away . . . The shuttle landed right on the edge of the line and I buried my face on the court.

The margin between victory and defeat proved to be the width of a line.

As I left the court, distraught, tears rolled down my cheeks and no words from my coach could console me. I quietly packed my kit and made my way out of the stadium.

'I have not seen people even double your age show this much courage.' Bhaiya held my hand and started the car to head back home.

Dad nodded in appreciation as he settled in the back seat with Mom. 'It was anybody's game, and you scared the hell out of her,' he agreed. 'You should be proud of yourself, beta.'

I looked out of the window, my eyes still moist.

'You are only thirteen, Payal, the youngest in the tournament. With age on your side, the Junior National Champion tag will be yours sooner than later!' Bhaiya consoled, patting my back.

'We'll see about that. Maybe this is a sign for her to get back to her studies,' Mom remarked.

'For the past two years, she has balanced her game with studies so well, Mom,' Bhaiya sounded irritated. 'Spending hours on court every day and still managing to keep pace with her studies is no mean feat. Moreover, haven't you seen her talent on the court? The coaches say . . .'

'I don't care what the coaches say,' Mom raised her voice. 'I don't want to see my daughter in pain and tears for a career that has a one-in-a-million chance of taking off!'

'Are you crazy, Mom?' Bhaiya matched her anger. 'She is already right up there . . . another good season and she could be the junior champion! Pain and hard work is part and parcel of the game!'

'Don't argue with me, Vaibhav, focus on the road,' Mom said in a cold voice.

Bhaiya must have felt that ignoring her was the best thing to do at that moment, so he turned to me.

'You should have attacked more on her backhand. And why didn't you drop more often?'

I spoke for the first time after the match.

'I was nervous. I knew what I had to do . . . I just could not execute it.'

'And why did you get so tired in the last game? Coach was happy about your fitness level till yesterday.' Dad sounded concerned.

'She had a fresher set of legs, Dad; I had to play two three-setters before reaching the finals!'

'Will you all stop this nonsense? Let's focus on getting her career in order, rather than discussing these silly matches!' Mom interrupted

'This is her life, Mom. Let's not . . .'

'Vaibhav, watch out!' Mom shrieked as a truck headed straight in our direction.

I was blinded by the headlights. Bhaiya swerved desperately to the left, but the truck hit our car from the other side and dragged us off the road. I screamed in horror as the car hit a big rock on the side of the road and somersaulted thrice before coming to a grinding halt upside down.

My door fell open and I was thrown out. My head hit the ground hard.

I remember seeing a stream of blood oozing out from the car, now a mangled mass of metal covered with shattered pieces of glass.

★ ★ ★

There was a smile on Bhabhi's lips as she read the newspaper, but a chill ran down my spine as the events of that night unfolded in my mind. Kavya looked enquiringly at me, and I forced a smile to reassure her.

Bhaiya and Mom had miraculously escaped with minor bruises. But Dad and I had bled profusely, and the thirty minutes that we spent in the ambulance had been the most excruciating time of my life. I had been semi-conscious, and vaguely remember Mom holding Dad's hand and controlling her tears, but finally breaking down at the hospital steps when he closed his eyes for ever.

Watching Dad breathe his last and me being rushed into the operation threatre simultaneously had been nerve-racking for *Bhaiya* and Mom. They told me later that it had seemed the end of the world when, two days later, the doctors informed them that due to my severe head injury, I had slipped into a coma.

Things finally brightened up for them when I came out of the coma after a month, and started recovering extremely well. Though I remained in the hospital for three months, our family had been given a new lease of life.

But it came at a cost.

The doctor told *Bhaiya* and Mom that I was suffering from a rare type of retrograde amnesia. I did not remember the last couple of years of my life—my struggle in badminton, my training, my tournaments and even the accident and Dad's death had been erased. I did not know that I was a professional badminton player. He concluded that I might get my memory back, but how long that would take was anybody's guess.

We shifted to Lucknow after I was discharged, and have lived there since then. No one told me about my professional badminton past, as Mom did not want the shadow of the game to fall on our family again—the sport that, according to her, had ruined my studies, ended Dad's life and nearly taken mine. She had undergone enough pain and torture, and had shown great courage in starting a new life for all of us. *Bhaiya* didn't want anything to upset her again and hence did not argue. As for me, I had only started playing badminton seriously two years back, so I didn't remember anything at all, other than that I liked playing the game. The news of Dad's death shattered me so much that I didn't even wonder about what else I could have lost.

And that's how my career ended prematurely.

I did play the sport occasionally after my recovery. The love for badminton was still very much alive in me. It was not only my favourite hobby, but also my stress buster. Alas . . . I had no clue what I had been and what I was capable of, like I do now. Mom was initially against my even picking up the racquet, and relented only after Bhaiya pleaded with her. She was also more lenient towards me after the accident, and therefore acquiesced, as long as it remained just a hobby.

The next three years passed uneventfully and I guess we all made peace with our fate in our own ways.

But on a rainy evening early last year, my life started to show the first signs of changing its colours once again.

We had been expecting Bhaiya and Bhabhi for dinner that evening.

2

A question of passion

'Why is it called shuttlecock, Mom?' It was an innocent question that simply popped into my mind as I watched Saina Nehwal battle Wang Yihan. But Mom was in no mood to satiate my thirst for badminton knowledge.

'I am too busy to answer your silly questions, Payal,' she replied and continued flipping through the pages of Tarla Dalal's latest offering. 'Why don't you help me lay the table? And can you please switch off the idiot box so that I can focus on getting this house in order before they arrive?'

It might have been Saina's most important match, but in this little house she had to concede to Tarla Dalal, and I to my mother's orders. Any hope of that question being answered was lost to the bigger issue that Mom now raised.

'Should we go for fruit custard or an apple pie for dessert?'

Resigned to my fate, I joined her in the preparations. After all, family dinners had become battlegrounds for culinary supremacy in our household since Bhaiya got married and moved to the other side of town.

While laying the table I glanced at my reflection in a glass cabinet nearby. Though I wasn't as pretty as Bhabhi,

I liked the way my long hair fell neatly on my back. 'Why does Kavya keep pestering me to cut my hair short?' I wondered.

Watching Mom's anxiety in the kitchen made me smile as my mind conjured up the exact words Dad would have said, had he been there. 'Payal beta, will you please tell Mom to stop panicking like the Indian team in the slog overs and start getting ready?'

I missed him.

Dad had been a sportsman at heart. In his heyday, he had opened the innings for his district and bowled tidy spells of leg-breaks. He had played cricket at the district level for three years during college and was on the verge of being selected to the Ranji team, when his budding career had been cut short by my grandparents.

'Cricket, ha! It's a good pastime, but how can you even think of making a career out of it? Do some real work, beta,' Dad was warned.

So that's what he had done. He had joined a big corporate house and gone on to become a very successful senior executive, but I had often seen him look longingly at the pitch in the stadium near our old house.

It was half past six when the bell rang. I opened the door and gave Bhaiya and Bhabhi a warm hug.

'So, big brother, the police called. They say you have been stealing all the food in the city. Look at you bloating up!'

'Very funny!' Bhaiya replied. 'This is all puppy fat, will go away very soon.'

'Puppy fat my foot! No one can say that you were a 100 m sprinter at one point. Look at Bhabhi, so slim and graceful. What do people say when they see you—Laurel and Hardy walking together?'

'People will say that young girls nowadays don't even offer water to the elders of the house,' he taunted me in turn and walked off to the kitchen.

Vishakha Bhabhi was indeed a gorgeous damsel who had swept Bhaiya off his feet with her surreal beauty the very first time he had seen her. Slender, fair, brown eyes, silky hair and a mesmerizing smile, why on earth did she fall for my brother!

I chatted with Bhabhi while Bhaiya rummaged through the fridge to find something palatable. Bhabhi was wearing a crisp green saree that highlighted her slim figure, and a black serpentine designer bindi, now her trademark. We got along very well. In fact, when she had come to our house after her marriage two years ago, nervous and anxious as most brides are, it was I who had put her at ease instantly. Perhaps in me she had found a friend, someone she could relate to and with whom she could share things that she would not even tell Bhaiya.

The evening became lively as we all gossiped away to glory.

'So Payal, how did your entrance exams go?' Bhaiya enquired after a while. He had been away on tours lately and had a lot to catch up on.

For a second, time froze. Everyone stopped talking. It seemed to me that even the birds stopped chirping and the wind came to a standstill.

I gave him a dirty look and remained silent. Mom conveniently shifted her gaze so as to avoid direct eye contact with anyone.

Finally, Bhabhi came to everyone's rescue.

'Now Payal, I know that you hate talking about this subject and it's the last thing that should be discussed on such a nice evening. But your bhaiya has a valid question, dear. You can't avoid this topic for long, can you? It concerns your career, after all.'

'Oh yes, my career! The sheer essence of life, the sole means of survival for mankind, with the entire human race waiting with bated breath trying to guess what my next career move will be; after all, the livelihood of millions of poor souls depends on what I choose to do with my life!' I retorted in such a caustic tone while making funny faces that Bhaiya couldn't help smiling.

'Yeah, yeah, you can afford to smile,' I continued when I noticed him. 'Your life is all hunky-dory with a beautiful wife and a steady job. What would you know about a poor girl like me!'

'Enough, Payal,' thundered Mom. 'You don't need to be so sarcastic. Bhaiya asked you a simple question and if you don't like answering it, then just say so directly. Why make such a fuss?'

'I'm sorry Mom, but I am so sick of discussing my career plans! If someone even mentions the word "career" now, I am going to puke all over your apple pie. So for the pie's sake, can we please change the topic?'

They decided not to spoil the evening and Mom's apple pie, and we went back to chatting as if nothing had happened.

After the sumptuous meal, everyone settled down in the living room but I headed straight for my room. After a while, there was a gentle knock on the door. Even before opening it, I knew it could be only one person.

'Not now, Bhaiya, you can scold me tomorrow.'

Bhaiya didn't seem upset. Instead he asked me gently, 'Now what has disturbed you so much that you won't even talk to me, your best friend?' Despite our six-year age gap, he indeed was my closest buddy.

There was a brief pause as I looked out of the window. A whiff of fresh breeze played with my hair. I closed my eyes, took a deep breath and asked, 'Why didn't you join the Indian Air Force, Bhaiya?'

For a second, he looked blank.

'You see,' I turned and looked at him now, 'for the last one year, all I have been asked by everyone—you all, my friends, teachers and even complete strangers—is how my preparations for the exams are going and what my plan is if I don't make it to IIT. I ignored it initially, then it started getting irritating, and now it makes me plain angry.'

I had recently given my 12th Boards, but had spent more time preparing for the IIT entrance exam. I had never been very keen to take the test, but Mom had convinced me that I was good and had what it took to crack the exam. I had obediently done what was expected of me.

'Why is this exam the cornerstone of success for every soul in this country? Why is it considered to be my career-defining moment? And forget the exam for a second, has anyone even asked me what I want to do in life? Do I even want to enter those hallowed portals if I clear the paper?'

Bhaiya remained silent.

'So tell me, why didn't you join the air force?'

It was now his turn to gaze out of the window. The cool breeze passed through the room, jingling Dad's medals hanging on the wall.

Bhaiya's eyes had a faraway look. I knew he was thinking of the other kind of medals that used to thrill him—the ones worn by dashing IAF pilots. The air force had fascinated him since his childhood. The charm of the uniform, the thrill of conquering the skies, the pride of protecting the nation—there was nothing more exciting to him than a career in the services.

But he, too, had been brainwashed into believing that he was meant for better things, capable of joining top institutes, undertaking the toughest of courses and as a result, earning potloads of money in the private sector.

I knew it had not been the money that had enticed him; it was just that he was weak. And that's why my question had pinched him deep inside.

'You know the answer, then why do you ask?' he replied in a low voice.

'I'm sorry, but I want you to see my point.'

When he did not reply, I continued, 'Do you remember the forlorn look in Dad's eyes whenever he visited the stadium to watch a match?'

'I see where you are going, Payal, but hang on. Dad was very happy with the way his career shaped up, and so am I with mine. Everybody makes little adjustments in life . . . so did we.'

'Little adjustments? Ha!' I gave him a sarcastic smile. 'Who are you kidding? Two people in my house who have compromised on their dreams to do what the world wanted them to do! Don't get me wrong, Bhaiya. I appreciate and admire what both of you have achieved. But can you deny the fact that you sacrificed your true calling, and will always regret it, deep down inside?'

As I paused to gulp down some water, I knew Bhaiya was figuring out a way to tackle me. Sure enough, after a while he remarked, 'Fair enough. But then tell me, what is it that you want to do in life? What is your passion, your dream?'

And there he had it. He must have known that I wouldn't have an answer to this.

He held my hand and said, 'Payal, I am glad that you're thinking all this. It will help you understand yourself better. But you still need to search deeper within your soul to find an answer to this question.'

With that, he kissed me gently on the forehead and left the room.

That night, I could not sleep. I had weird dreams. I was standing next to Pullela Gopichand and asking him why a shuttlecock was called thus. And the very next moment, I had turned into a shuttlecock and was being tossed from one court to another, first a court full of engineers, the next full of doctors, another one of lawyers . . . and everyone was laughing at me, signalling to me to keep quiet and enjoy getting tossed.

I woke up with a start.

'I need a break,' I sighed.

3

A breath of fresh air

The next morning, I hurriedly finished my breakfast and left the house, hailing a rickshaw.

The traffic in Lucknow is one of a kind. Cycle rickshaws, bicycles, handcarts, bikes, autorickshaws, tempos, buses, Marutis, Hondas, swanky SUVs and the most prominent of all, the black beauty, the omnipresent buffalo—all of them can be seen jostling for space on the narrow roads of the city. The buffalo is truly the queen here. You can find one taking a dip in the Gomti river; lazing around right in the middle of a traffic hold-up, as if supervising the cop; walking alongside college dudes on the streets of Hazratganj—she's the glue that holds this city together!

I asked the rickshaw-walla to stop in front of Pizza Hut. Dressed in a frilly pink top over a denim skirt, my best friend Kavya was busy chatting with a young trainee waiter at the entrance. Her big, black eyes shone brightly, as she intermittently ran her fingers through her short, wavy and streaked hair. Though slightly chubby, her charming personality never failed to attract attention wherever she went.

'May I interrupt?' I tapped her shoulder from behind.

'Hey Pihu, finally I get to see you!' Kavya turned around, jumped with joy and hugged me. As she did so, her hands hit the tray that the waiter was holding and all the glasses came crashing down!

Everyone stopped eating and looked up, making me go red with embarrassment. But Kavya was undaunted.

'Oh! Sorry, dude,' she told the waiter and bent to help him clean up the mess. The waiter, however. politely refused her help and pointed us to our table.

She turned back, hugged me once more and we both took the table near the big glass window of the restaurant, from which one could see the buffaloes sitting just outside, chewing their meals in peace.

'So my busy bee, where have you been? And why are there dark circles under your eyes? And why aren't you wearing those cool red sandals of yours that you love so much? And how are Bhaiya-Bhabhi doing? Oh gosh, we have so much to catch up on!'

I smiled at her. The sun was shining brightly but the tinted glass window shaded us from the rays. I was sitting with my best friend, listening to her non-stop chatter in my favourite restaurant with my favourite music playing in the background. Everything seemed just right. I felt relaxed for the first time after the turmoil of the previous night.

'Look over there, Pihu. See how that aunty is trying to impress her NRI son-in-law by struggling to eat the pizza with fork and knife.'

'How do you know that he is her son-in-law and an NRI?'

'Well, while I was waiting for you, there was nothing to do till I met that cute waiter.' Kavya winked. 'So I just sat near their table and eavesdropped, trying to find some excitement in life,' she giggled.

That's Kavya for you. The most cheerful girl I had ever known. She was always full of life, bubbling with energy. She spoke incessantly, lived life to the fullest and I had never seen her without a smile on her face.

Kavya was known for her weirdness as well. Once she went white-water rafting at Rishikesh and came back with her hair fully shaved off. 'It just gets so hot in Lucknow during summers, you see,' she explained matter-of-factly. On another occasion, she forced me to join a random baraat on the road, dancing along with the groom's friends. She entered the wedding in style with a garland around her neck, ate one of the most lavish wedding dinners ever, and slipped out confidently as I followed in horror and embarrassment.

I loved her company. I guess, deep inside, I wanted to be like her—fun-loving and carefree, following my heart all the way.

'So Kuhu, how's college life?'

Kavya was studying physics at Isabella Thoburn, better known as I.T. College. She had finished school last year and had always wanted to pursue pure sciences. Luckily for her, there was no opposition from her dad. However, knowing Kavya, she would have climbed to the top of the Imambara and threatened to jump off if forced to study anything against her wish!

'College is rocking. The electrons are behaving well, chai at the cafeteria is hot and steamy and Professor Mehra is looking more dashing by the day!' she replied with a naughty smile. 'I can't tell you how much I missed your company while you were sulking in your books, Pihu. I am so glad your exams are over. I want to spend this entire vacation with you; I don't know where you will be headed after that. I hope you get Kanpur; at least you'll be close by.'

My face started losing its colour as Kavya looked at me enquiringly. I narrated the conversation I had had with Bhaiya the night before and ended by telling her about the weird dream.

'See Pihu, I really don't know how I can help you find out your true calling in life,' she remarked after hearing me out. After pausing to sip her Pepsi, she continued, 'But why don't we forget all this now and have some fun today? I might not be able to solve your problems, but I can provide you with something that you desperately need right now—a change! Let's just have an evening of P–K fun together, to hell with everything else.'

The sun had started to set as we went out, colouring the sky in a weird shade of orange. The call for prayer could be heard from a faraway mosque. Hazratganj had just started to light up to its full glory and the by-lanes were slowly getting filled up with people of all generations. Children were spoilt for choices, unable to decide if they should settle for a sugar candy or a balloon, or try their luck bargaining with their parents for both. Young couples could be seen hand-in-hand, the girl checking out trinkets at the roadside stalls and the boy trying to prove that he was no novice when it came to street shopping. Dads and moms were busy shopping for groceries, with the moms stopping in front of every shoe store window to check out the latest designs. Ice-cream and kulfi carts, bhutta sellers, chaat stalls, bhelpuri wallas—there was no dearth of options for a tempting evening snack. Most of the shops were lit up with small fairy lights, creating infinite designs as they went on and off. It looked like the entire city had descended on the streets of Ganj to enjoy their weekend evening.

The setting was just perfect to enliven my mood. It's tough not to feel happy after experiencing Ganj at its cheerful best. Add to that company like Kavya's, and you have the perfect recipe for a lovely evening.

On the way back, I sat smiling to myself in the rickshaw. Kavya had made me forget all my worries and Ganj had never been so enticing before. I was in a state of bliss and was certain that at least that night I would sleep soundly, without a care in the world.

★ ★ ★

'Wake up Payal, it's Kavya on the phone. And look at the clock; it's 10 a.m.' Mom shook me out of my sleep, handing me the phone.

'Um . . . hm . . . hello . . .' I muttered sleepily, my eyes still closed.

'Pihu baby, I have some exciting news for us,' Kavya said in a rush.

'It's so early in the morning, Kuhu. Can't you let me sleep in peace?'

'I am coming over to your house in half an hour. We will talk in detail then. Tell aunty to cook lunch for me.'

'Talk in detail about what?' I was now thoroughly confused.

Kavya seemed to be in a hurry, so she quickly put the phone down. True to her words, she arrived right on time and came straight to my room.

'You said you wanted a break from everything, right?' she shouted as she came in. 'Some time away from all the worries? I have just the perfect plan for both of us!'

'Will you stop talking in riddles and come straight to the point please?' I replied, still feeling sleepy.

'I was chatting with Vishakha Bhabhi yesterday night. She had called to ask about my mom's health. She was telling me about how her friend is shifting to Pune, and then we started talking about Pune and how great that place is for youngsters and how beautiful the scenic hill spots around it are . . .'

'Come to the point, Kuhu.' I was getting restless.

'The point is, we have lots of holidays remaining, and we need to get you out of this city so that you can relax completely and recharge your batteries!'

'And so you propose that . . .' I deliberately left the sentence unfinished.

'Yup. Let's get the hell out of here!' Kavya jumped on my bed. 'Let's go to Pune. My mausi's family stays there, remember? They are so affectionate and would love to have us stay with them. Also, the city is surely livelier than Lucknow. Many of our friends have gone there to study, so we will have good company. Then there are so many places nearby where we can have mini holidays in turn—Bombay, Lonavala, Khandala—and we can actually plan a visit to Goa as well! I can't see any better place to spend our vacations.'

I was deep in thought. Pune, the city where I was born and where I had lived when I was small . . . we had shifted from there a few years later, following Dad's transfer.

'What are you thinking, girl?' Kavya said, poking my arm. 'What are you going to do sitting at home for the next two months? And all that gibberish about your "passion in life" and your "true calling" will simply eat your head. You need fresh air, and this is your chance to get that.'

'Don't call it gibberish,' I snapped. 'I really mean it.'

'Okay, okay, I'm sorry. But let's not digress. Let's talk to Aunty right away. We don't have much time.'

Convincing Mom proved to be much simpler than we had envisaged. She was just glad that I was getting a much-needed break to sort out my mind.

And so it was decided. We were to leave for Pune in exactly one week. Tickets and other administrative tasks were outsourced to Bhaiya, and he was more than glad to assist.

The night before our departure, I gave him a call. 'Bhaiya, I just want to apologize for the way I spoke to you that evening. It was very rude on my part. You have always been my biggest strength, and there is no justification for the way I behaved.'

'Oh Payal, forget it,' Bhaiya said, cheerful as always. 'You were troubled and all you did was pour your heart out to me. I am just happy that you are going for a nice break.'

'I hope so. And I will shop a lot for Bhabhi and bring her some nice Osho chappals,' I said with a cheer in my voice that had been missing for quite some time.

'Hahaha! You think you will get away with just the chappals? Think again, madam. You are soon going to get a call from her with the big shopping list she has been preparing since morning!'

Kavya and I left by train the next evening. Bhaiya couldn't come to the station to see us off, but I'm sure he must have prayed for our safe journey.

Little did any of us know how this trip would completely change our lives in the days to come.

4

A champ in the making

'Aren't train journeys such fun, Pihu? I feel like our vacation has already started!' Kavya was at her cheerful best as she looked out of the tinted glass window of our air-conditioned compartment.

She was right. We were enjoying this experience to its fullest. The train passed through diverse terrains, winding down the hillocks of Madhya Pradesh and crossing Maharashtra. The earth looked green in patches and despite the scorching summer, the calm blue lakes were full. Village after village came and went. A bunch of scantily-clad kids jumped and waved at the train as their fathers toiled in the fields.

Oblivious to their hardships, we were sitting in the cool confines of our compartment, the filtered rays from the sun providing just enough warmth to make it a beautiful and lazy afternoon. I gazed out of the window, soaking in the beauty of Mother Nature. Kavya, on the other hand, was praying that the guy sitting opposite would start a conversation with us. After all, the first thing she had done after boarding the train was to check out all the 'M-19 to M-25' names on the reservation chart! She had worn a triumphant grin ever since she found out that one such 'target' was sitting right inside our compartment.

Either the guy sensed Kavya's intentions or he was himself a proponent of the 'reservation chart' strategy, for he looked up at her.

'Are you girls going to Pune?' he asked.

'Where else is this train supposed to go, you dodo?' I mentally muttered; I didn't like the fact that someone had disturbed the blissful peace inside the cabin.

But Kavya jumped at her good fortune and replied with a wide smile, 'Yes, we are on a holiday. I am Kavya and she's my friend Payal.'

'They call me Gaurav,' he smiled back.

'So, do you live in Pune or are you also a visitor like us?' Kavya continued.

'I work at Infosys there. I completed my graduation in agricultural sciences last year from Pune itself.'

My irritation levels rising, I blurted, 'Agriculture to IT, eh? How did you end up losing focus?'

Kavya glared at my acerbic remark.

'It's not about losing focus,' Gaurav replied, unruffled. 'I got a good opportunity and simply grabbed it.'

'So you mean whenever you get any good opportunities in life, you will grab them, irrespective of where your expertise lies, what your dreams are?' I shot back.

I realized I was being rude to him, but he kept his cool.

'See, at the end of the day, I am happy with what I am doing,' he said, his smile intact. 'So I will keep grabbing good opportunities in life as long as I am happy with what I do.'

'But isn't it more important to do what makes you happy than to be happy with what you do?' I wondered aloud.

It was a profound question indeed. In fact, it was only when I said it that I realized this was probably the very thing that had been bothering me for the past few days.

'All right, enough of philosophy! Pihu, let's grab a bite before I die of hunger,' Kavya suddenly interrupted my thoughts. She got up, her patience clearly running out. I quietly followed her to the pantry car.

★ ★ ★

'So, you like to play tennis?' I heard a male voice say as we crossed the compartment just before the pantry.

'Not really. I just play casually and watch a bit on TV, that's all,' came a girl's reply. I was about to move on but stopped in my tracks at her next sentence. 'By the way, this is a badminton racquet.' This mention of the sport made me turn around to look at the berth from where the two voices had originated.

My eyes rested on a girl pointing to the racquet next to her—she was tall, extremely slim, wheatish, with short, curly hair and a disregard for fashion, judging by her clothes; she looked ordinary at best.

A little intrigued now, I signalled to Kavya to stand at the compartment's door for a while, from where I could hear the conversation clearly. She resisted at first but quickly gave up and started fiddling with her iPod.

The boy sitting opposite the short-haired girl continued, 'Oh yes, of course it is. I used to play badminton for my college. What a great sport, so athletic and fast! I follow it more keenly than cricket.'

The girl smiled. 'Oh really . . . so who is your favourite player?'

'Peter Gade,' he said confidently.

'Oh, what a coincidence! He's my favourite too. So what do you like the most about his game?' she persisted and I could see him getting slightly uncomfortable.

'Umm . . . I like his all-round game, he's a good athlete . . .' he stopped abruptly, as if not knowing what to say next.

'But what do you think makes him so different from the Asian players?'

'I think Asian players are as good as him. Gopichand is a good match for him, I am sure.'

I couldn't control my laughter and was not surprised when the girl shot back, 'Gopichand? He retired from badminton long back, while Peter is still going strong. When I mentioned Asian players, I was talking more about the likes of Lin Dan and Lee Chong Wei.'

He looked at her blankly.

'Actually, I think Peter's strength lies primarily in his deceptive shots and his full-strength slice smashes,' she continued. 'His flick serve is the perfect example of this deception. I have also seen him implement this deception on his net game. Even though he is able to take the shuttle at net height, he still decides to let it drop and then plays it just before it touches the floor, thus surprising the opponent and delaying his reaction. Even Camilla Martin, the other great Danish champion, was a big proponent of these deception shots. It's sad that the Asian champs have started to use it frequently as their weapon only recently.'

The entire cabin was silent now, staring at this girl incredulously. The boy's face, on the other hand, clearly showed that he would have liked to jump off the train to prevent further embarrassment.

I had started to enjoy this, and the girl was on a roll now. She decided to end his misery with a final blow.

'As for his other strength, if you remember the All England 2004 finals, Gade used his full-strength slice smashes or the fast drops, as you may call them, to great effect against Lin Dan. He would smash the shuttle using full strength, slice it in such a way that it travelled full speed till the net. Once it crossed over, it slowed down drastically and died just near the service line, leaving Dan flummoxed. But Gade could never get the Olympic gold. I wonder if . . .'

Probably unable to face the humiliation any longer, the boy cut her short, 'Excuse me. I need to go to the washroom.'

She sat there smiling as he left.

'Why don't they just stick to cricket instead of trying to impress a girl with some crap about a sport they don't even know! Anyway, it was good fun,' I remarked to Kavya, just loud enough for the girl to hear.

She looked up at us for the first time. Her eyes were gleaming.

'He probably thought that a guy with knowledge on any other sport than cricket would be unique . . . and then the chances of a girl knowing something concrete about badminton was one in a thousand, I guess!' She laughed and removed her racquet from the berth, making space for us to sit.

'I guess Peter's was the only international name he had ever heard on TV . . . possibly while flipping channels to watch a cricket match!' I laughed. 'I am sure he is cursing himself right now for choosing the wrong topic to impress you.' I had now settled down next to her, and Kavya had no choice but to follow suit.

The girl extended her hand cordially. 'I am Sakshi.'

'I'm Payal, and this is my friend Kavya.'

The next hour passed in a flash as the three of us chatted like long-lost buddies.

Born in Nagpur, Sakshi had been living in Lucknow with her aunt, Sharmila Kapoor, since she was four. She was the only family Sakshi had. Mrs Kapoor was a teacher while Sakshi had just given her BA first-year exams. But what was most fascinating about this girl was the fact that for years, she had been nurturing a dream, a passion that made her far more focused, more mature and stronger than most girls of her age—she dreamt of playing badminton for the country.

She had been playing the game since she was a kid. When all her classmates would go to the park to play hide-and-seek, or watch TV or simply hang around, Sakshi would be sweating it out on the badminton court, aiming to beat opponents double her age. Her aunt had noticed her talent early and had got her professional coaching. However, after Mr Kapoor passed away, the coaching had had to stop, due to financial constraints. But Sakshi continued training on her own and started participating in competitions. She had captained her school badminton team in various inter-school competitions in Lucknow, and had already won four gold medals by the time she graduated from school. She had not been able to represent Lucknow University, though, due to a bout of malaria.

She used to tutor kids in her colony so that she could at least sustain her badminton, reducing the burden on her aunt. It was with this hard-earned money that she had treated herself to a brand-new Yonex racquet on her birthday this year. She could not afford the best one in the market, but she had no regrets.

'So why are you going to Pune? Do you have relatives there?' I asked, already admiring her vision and courage.

'A coaching camp. It is one of the biggest in the country. After two months of training, the top players will be identified as future potentials and selected to train further for the district team. Then the state selection tournaments and finally, the nationals!'

'Wow!' It was Kavya's turn now to be impressed.

'It is the best stepping stone for me.'

'Your aunt must be so proud of you!' I smiled.

Sakshi suddenly grew pensive. 'Yeah, she is . . .' After a pause, she continued, 'Today, she was giving me instructions till the last minute, standing on the platform next to my window. Her eyes had so much love and affection for me. I really want to return as a champion and do my aunt proud.' Her voice choked a little, and she turned away from us to gaze out of the window.

Kavya patted Sakshi's back lightly and broke the trance.

'You are a strong girl, Sakshi,' she said. Then on a lighter note, 'And please give me your autograph right now—god only knows if you'll even remember us once you become a hotshot player!'

Sakshi smiled a little. Kuhu had changed the mood, as always.

I looked at Sakshi with admiration. She knew what she wanted out of life. She had wings and she wanted to fly. She was all that I was not.

I wanted her to win, and said a silent prayer for her.

5

New beginnings

I was still a bit sleepy as we stepped on to the platform at Pune railway station early morning next day. There was a pleasant chill in the air, but we knew it would become hotter as the day progressed. When we called, we were told that Kavya's aunt and uncle had just reached the parking lot, so we hurriedly picked up our bags and rushed out.

After quick introductions, we drove off, giving Sakshi a lift to her guest house.

'So, Mausi, how's Lyka doing?'

'Well, you can see for yourself on reaching home,' Kavya's aunt replied as the car zoomed off.

As soon as we entered the house, a one-year-old Labrador latched on to Kavya in a flash. This must be Lyka! Kavya adored dogs and even I had to admit that Lyka was one of the cutest pups I had seen. Kavya spent the first five minutes playing and making friends with her. I, on the other hand, was indifferent. Lyka did sniff me for a short time but then went back to Kavya.

We spent the entire day relaxing and chatting with our hosts. Mausi was quite fashionable—with her stylishly cut shoulder-length curly hair, pretty pink pearl earrings, a slick gemstone necklace and a designer salwar-kurta, she could have given stiff competition to girls half her age. She was also well travelled and well read, which made her fun to talk to. But most importantly, she was an excellent cook, loved experimenting with exotic dishes and had already prepared a list of delicacies that she was going to pamper us with. She also enjoyed gossiping, and was looking forward to discussing all the family members and recent marriages with Kavya.

'So, girls, what's the plan?' Mausaji, Kavya's uncle, asked after we had settled down in the living room, post a hearty meal.

'Well, we had thought of meeting two of our former classmates. They were supposed to be our guide to the city. But we just found out that they had to go to Bombay for three–four days. So I guess till then, we will just relax,' Kavya said, stretching on the couch.

Before Mausaji could reply, the doorbell rang. Mausi opened the door and in came a tall, slim boy, sporting a black Bob Dylan T-shirt and black trousers, with a satchel on his shoulder. The dimpled smile on his face, along with his slicked-back hair and a slight stubble, made him look quite handsome.

'Hey Adi beta, come in. How are you?' Mausaji got up and beamed.

'I'm good, Uncle, but in a bit of a hurry. Dad has sent these for you.' The boy held out a sheaf of papers.

Mausaji turned to us and said, 'Girls, this is Aditya Prabhakar. My friend's son.'

'Hi. You can call me Adi,' he said with a smile.

As Kavya was lost in admiring his looks, I introduced us. We chatted briefly and then Adi got up to leave.

'I guess your friend doesn't speak much,' he said mischievously to me.

Kavya went red, and could only mutter the words, 'Nothing like that.'

'Adi, till their friends are back in town, maybe you can show them around. That would be more exciting for them than staying at home with oldies like us.' Mausaji laughed and looked at Kavya. She nodded silently, her eyes downcast.

'Sounds great!' Adi smiled. 'Uncle, you will go to Kothrud to meet Dad tomorrow, right? You can drop them on your way at the sports complex at 12. I should be done by then.'

With that, Adi left and we went to our room after thanking Mausaji.

I had been waiting desperately to pull Kavya's leg.

'The most talkative girl I know getting tongue-tied! Adi's aura, haan?'

The naughty twinkle in Kavya's eyes said it all. She winked at me. 'I think these holidays are going to be one hell of an exciting ride,' she grinned and both of us laughed.

★ ★ ★

At 11.30 the next morning, Kavya and I stood at the entrance of the City Sports Complex, waiting for our new friend. But Adi was nowhere to be seen, and as we stepped towards a bench under the shade, a tall girl bumped into us.

'Oh my god . . . I didn't know Pune is so small,' I exclaimed as I looked up at her in surprise.

Sakshi laughed and asked, 'What are you girls doing here?'

'We came to meet a friend, but can't see him around.'

'Come in. He should be on one of the courts.'

As we entered the complex, I was enthralled by the sheer size of the hall. Ten badminton courts were lined up next to each other, their shining wooden floors and freshly painted lines perfect enough to satisfy even connoisseurs of the game. Huge floodlights lit up the entire hall and long staircases circumscribed the courts to ensure maximum seating capacity. A smaller adjoining hall contained the lockers, showers and water coolers. The entire hall smelt of fresh wood. The place looked grand and I loved it.

'I am sorry, girls; the programme for the day got delayed!' Adi tapped my shoulder from behind and said.

Kavya, prepared to confront her dream guy this time, was nonchalant. 'Oh, that's okay. We can wait, no problem.' I knew that deep inside, she was looking forward to seeing him play.

'Sportsmen are so sexy,' she sighed as Adi strode off.

I winked at her and sighed back, 'Oh, the thrills of love at first sight!'

'Shhh,' Kavya nudged me. Standing in front of a large group of youngsters was a man in his early thirties, waiting for the crowd to settle down. He was dressed immaculately in a white T-shirt and track pants, and his face was devoid of any emotion.

'There are two kinds of people amongst all of you here today,' he finally spoke, his voice loud, clear and firm. Everyone was quiet now. 'Those who want to improve their game and take it one notch higher, and those for whom this game is their life, their dream, their passion and probably their career. But all of you share something in common. Can anyone tell me what that is?'

'Our love for the game,' came a voice from behind.

'Precisely. So if there is someone who is here for any reason other than this, he or she may please leave now. I want to spend my next two months with a group that loves the game so much, it's willing to spend six hours every day on these courts and still end up wanting more.'

There was no sound, no movement.

'Guys and girls, my name is Purab and I am the head coach of this camp.'

I looked intently at him. For a moment I felt I had seen him before . . . I racked my brains for a while and then dismissed the thought.

'All of you will be split into two groups—intermediate and expert. Coaching for both groups will run in parallel, though with separate methods. But today, you will all play together since the coaches will first see everyone's game before finalizing the groups.'

The thunder of shuttles suddenly enveloped the huge hall as everyone began playing. I loved the sweet sound of the shuttle hitting the racquet strings—it was music to my ears, something that had always calmed my nerves when I was restless. The action all around me made me smile.

Thump!

Sakshi's feet made a loud noise on the wooden floor every time she landed. Her smashes flew like bullets and her movements were as swift as a deer's. To see a young girl from the same town as mine stamping her authority over these other professional-looking players gave me a sense of pride.

By the time Sakshi left the court, she was drenched in sweat but her face bore a gleaming smile.

'Did you play the game in your past life too?' I teased her.

'Hahaha! I don't know about that. But I do know that I want to spend this birth playing as long as I can. By the way, where is your friend?'

I threw a glance at the other court where Kavya was watching Adi play. As he finished his game, she beamed at him and gushed, 'You are so good!'

'Ah, not really. I am no professional; just here to sharpen my game,' he smiled.

'You cover the court well, Adi,' I commented as I joined them. 'But you jump a bit early to hit your smashes and lose balance and thus, power and direction.'

'Wow. Spot on! The coach pointed out the same issue.'

I smiled while Kavya glared at me.

'Do you play?' Adi asked me.

'Yeah . . . sometimes. I love the game. But it's been quite a while now.'

After a momentary silence, he asked me, 'Do you want to knock around a bit with me while all the players take a break?'

I shrugged my shoulders. 'Well . . . sure. It will be fun.'

It felt good to be on the court. However, five minutes into our play, I noticed the head coach watching us from the sidelines.

I started to feel a slight tingling sensation and trembled a little. Not that I was there to compete; but I always took pride in my game and wanted to be seen as a player who knew it a bit better than others. My palms started sweating and it seemed as if the racquet would slip from my hand any time. My feet were dragging and my shots were very tentative. I slowly started to panic, missing simple shots and finding the net more often than anyone should.

Before things could get worse, Sakshi came to my rescue.

'Hey Payal, why don't you break for five minutes?' She looked at Purab at the same time and he nodded in the affirmative.

I came off the court, sweating, and looked for some water to cool down.

Sakshi looked at me intently. 'Listen Payal, I am sorry for butting in like this. But it pains me to see a good player putting up a shoddy display only because of mental pressure.'

'How do you know that I am a better player?' I asked, despondent.

'Well, there are a lot of indicators—the way you hold your racquet and bend your shoulder while hitting shots, the way your wrists move when you drop the shuttle, the way you take steps on the court instead of running, the way you try to play as close to the lines as possible . . .'

I inclined my head.

'No one is judging you. So why are you making such a big deal out of it? Just play naturally and enjoy!'

'Maybe that's my thing—I always over-complicate stuff and have a nervous breakdown as a result,' I muttered to myself as the events of the past few days at home flashed through my mind. Then I turned to Kavya and said, 'Anyway, let's leave, Kuhu. They will take more time. We can shop and meet them for lunch after they are done.'

I didn't want to play any further. Kavya was reluctant to leave the stadium without Adi, but the shopping bait worked.

A couple of hours later, the four of us were sitting and sipping cool coconut water at a place bustling with college students and young couples.

'This is Vaishali Restaurant,' Adi told us. 'It's one of the oldest and most popular hangouts in Pune. You will always find it buzzing with a hip crowd.' He was clearly relishing his role as our guide.

In the short time that he spent with us, he also told us all about himself. He was quite similar to Kavya when it came to chatting non-stop. He was studying English literature at one of the city's best colleges. But what caught my interest was the fact that his father was in the Indian Air Force.

'So Adi, you live at the air force base, right? Our home in Lucknow is also near one. My brother had always wanted to join the air force. I used to wonder what was so special in that job; it's so risky!'

'Okay, first, it's not a job. It's so much more than that,' Adi said, sounding a little hurt. After a short pause, something struck him and he continued, 'In fact, why don't you guys come see it for yourselves sometime? That will be the best way Payal can figure out why her brother longed for this career.'

'Sounds like a great idea.' Kavya was the first one to jump at the suggestion; it meant spending more time with Adi!

That night I had a weird dream. Bhaiya was flying a twin-seat fighter jet and I was sitting in the rear seat with Kavya. I asked him to stop the plane near a cloud, where we got down to play badminton with Purab and Adi. However, Kavya and Adi flew to a nearby cloud for some privacy and sipped coconut water together while I was left to face Purab alone. I kept flying all around the court to reach every corner where Purab hit the shuttle. Bhaiya cheered me on, stopping the plane in mid-air to watch the game. I was laughing, loving the way I was flying and making Purab run on the cloud. Bhaiya waved at me, joining me in my laughter. But just then, the plane lost balance and started to hurtle towards the ground. I watched in horror, and started crying.

'Noo!' I got up with a shriek, sweating profusely. My eyes were moist. Kuhu was in deep slumber and I decided not to wake her up. I sat on the bed for some time, then got up, drank some water and looked at my watch. It was 3 a.m. I didn't care. I called up Bhaiya. He answered in a sleepy voice.

'Bhaiya, are you okay?' I asked frantically.

'Eh? What? Payal? What time is it? What's wrong?'

'Nothing, all is fine here. Just tell me if you are okay or not.'

'Of course I am. Why?'

'No reason. Go back to sleep, we'll talk tomorrow. I love you. Good night.'

There are times when you miss someone so much that you don't want to sleep, in the fear that you may stop thinking about that person. That was one such night for me.

6

The battle begins

'Move your fat legs quicker! You are not models walking on a ramp, I hope you know.'

Purab could get really nasty with his pupils, as I gradually discovered, but I was much more hurt on this occasion than on any of the others. Remarks on my badminton skills were fine, expected and actually required. 'But how could he comment on the one topic every girl on this planet is so sensitive about!' I muttered angrily to myself.

My mind flashed back to that day when Sakshi had called me up and requested me to come to the court. I was now regretting that I had agreed to that request.

'I want you to join the camp, Payal,' Purab had told me bluntly when I had reached, Kavya in tow.

I vividly remembered the surprise on both Kavya's face and mine.

Purab had continued, 'You are extremely talented, only rusty. I have seen numerous budding players in my career as a coach, but the talent that you have at your age is simply amazing. Yes, you struggled on court that day, but your basics are perfectly in place. Have you ever taken your game seriously?'

I had shaken my head, still unsure if that conversation was for real. This was the first time anyone had ever spoken to me seriously about my game, and I was loving every bit of it.

'If there is one thing that pains me, Payal, it is to see talent go waste. And so I want you to train with the group. You are not a professional, but I want you to get an opportunity to train like them and see what a transformed player you can become in two months.'

Surprised, shocked and elated, I had had no clue how to respond. It was Kuhu who had come to my rescue.

'It's not a bad idea actually. We are here for two months, in any case. Coaching would only take up a part of your time. The rest of the time we'll have fun! And then it will be a good learning experience for you.' Kavya's support was primarily due to her belief in my (supposed) talent, but I knew that part of the reason was the opportunity to spend more time in Adi's company.

I had seen no harm in the plan. It would be good exposure for me, and after all, I did love the game.

I had agreed . . . but now I cursed myself for that decision.

'Now Payal, go to the baseline and hit all your shots from there with such power that they reach the opposite baseline,' Purab instructed. 'For every shot that doesn't reach the opponent's back gallery, you will run one extra round of this stadium before the next class.'

I was gradually beginning to realize that professional coaching was no child's play. This was my third class and I was already burnt out. The entire group would start the day by performing various exercises to warm up. Each player would then be individually attended to by a coach, who would work with us on a particular aspect of the game—one focus area for each day. After taking a break for three hours, we would reassemble and follow a similar exercise routine as the morning to wake ourselves up from any lethargy that might have crept in. We would then break into groups and start playing actual matches with each other, under the watchful guidance of the coaches. Finally, the coaches would themselves play against us to ensure that their guidance was being implemented to perfection.

'Your shots are falling in the middle of the court instead of the back gallery, Payal,' Purab warned. 'The opponent will kill you if you do that in a match.'

'My arms are tiring, Purab, I know where and how to hit it but I just can't.' I started to feel helpless. 'Can I take a break, please?'

'I have seen immensely talented players fall by the wayside because their bodies were not ready for the challenge. And I have also seen seemingly average players perform miracles on court, simply due to the unbelievable limits they could push their bodies to.'

As Purab left to let me reflect on his statement, Kavya approached.

'Time for lunch, champ. And let's make it quick.' She paused and looked naughtily at me. 'I have a date today!'

'Excuse me?' My eyes widened. 'Did I hear you right?'

'Hahaha . . . yes you did. I have been invited for coffee and a bike ride to the Khadakvasla Lake in the evening. Now you tell me, only a fool will turn down such a charming offer, isn't it?'

Kavya could not stop giggling. I was amused, to say the least, but also extremely happy to see my friend in such high spirits.

'You are a clever little girl! Actually, Adi seems to be a nice guy.'

'Yeah, I know. I don't go out with "not nice" guys! Anyway, I need to have a glowing, radiant face when he comes to pick me up. So stop tiring me and let's go eat something. I may just pass out from hunger!'

Kavya was so cute and adorable! I gave her a tight hug.

'You are a darling, Kavya, I don't know what I would do without all your antics and buffoonery!'

* * *

Back in the stadium, Purab spotted me from afar and shouted, 'Payal! On the court, now! Let's get going with some practice matches.' Under normal circumstances, I would have loved to do as he said immediately. But at that instant, my enthusiasm vanished—the sight of my opponent gave me cold feet.

I started talking to myself as I bent down to tie my laces and pick up the racquet. 'Come on Payal, this is just a practice game. And everyone knows she's the best player in this camp. So just relax and enjoy.' My mind was trying its best to keep calm but my body was adamant not to listen to it. With trembling hands and sweaty palms, I walked towards the court. But before I could step on it, I saw Sakshi charging towards me from the opposite side agitatedly.

'What the hell is the matter with you?' she shouted.

I stared sheepishly. 'I am sorry.'

'On the contrary, *I* am sorry for *you*. Here you are, a perfectly good player, someone who actually loves the game. But what a pity, because when the time of action comes, you chicken out. Do you have absolutely no faith in your abilities?' Sakshi minced no words.

'I get a bit nervous. But once I settle down on court, I will slowly get back into rhythm.'

'By the time you get into your so-called "rhythm", I would have already finished you!'

'I know, and I'm trying my best to overcome this. With time, I will, you'll see!'

Sakshi smiled, having cooled down a bit now. As she walked back towards the other side of the court, she remarked, 'I think I have to become your psychiatrist during this camp—you are in dire need of counselling, and I do a good job.'

'I will be honoured,' I replied with a wink.

Both of us started off steadily, trying not to kill the shuttle early and engaging in rallies from the back gallery. Purab had told me he would monitor my feet movement very closely during the practice matches. Knowing him, he really didn't care which girl won the game. His only concern was to spot the flaws in our techniques and then devise improvement programmes to iron them out.

Five minutes into the game and Sakshi started to display why she was the best player around. Her smashes were kissing the sidelines and her precise drops kept me on my toes. Initially, I managed to respond quite well to Sakshi's onslaught. However, with every passing minute, she stepped up her game. I was confident by now, but after a point, I was just not able to match her power and stamina. Her aggression was too hot to handle!

The game got over quite quickly and we walked off the court, drenched in sweat.

'You are just incredible.' I was panting too much to say anything else at that moment.

As we got ready to leave later in the evening, I remarked, 'I wonder how Kavya's date is going.'

'Oh, she's with that charmer, is it?' Sakshi enquired.

I laughed, imagining Adi as a snake charmer, with Kavya slowly rising from a basket, swaying to his tunes.

After dinner, I went for a walk with Kavya to enjoy the cool night breeze. Lyka accompanied us as well. She was lazy to the core and hated it when we took her out to play with us. Kavya would throw a ball, goading Lyka to fetch it, but Lyka would simply give her a disdainful look and stroll lazily towards it. Then she would try to play with the ball but trip on it and fall down, again and again, before finally giving up and simply lying down beside it. It was evident that Lyka had grown extremely fond of Kavya. Whenever Kavya returned home, she would rush to the door and jump on her, wagging her tail eagerly in anticipation of being caressed. With me, though, she maintained a distance, as I did with her.

As soon as we were out, Kavya started rattling off every detail of her day. 'Pune is such a beautiful city!' She couldn't stop smiling.

'And Adi's company made it all the more appealing,' I teased her.

Her smile turned into laughter.

'What?' I enquired, smiling as well, and she animatedly took me through the events of the day.

He had asked her what she was doing, and at her response, told her that he considered physics a bit inconsistent with her personality.

'He said I am so bubbly, cheerful, naughty, stylish . . . and . . . umm, fun-loving, that physics seemed a rather dull stream for me.' Kavya's face was turning pink. 'He couldn't picture me sitting seriously for hours together in the lab, analyzing a pendulum swing.'

'So what did he expect you to do?' I enquired lazily.

'Something like fashion designing, mass communication or hotel management.'

'How clichéd!'

'No . . . he's cute! But I also turned the tables on him!'

I could see her eyes shining.

'I told him my dream was to support and carry forward the ground-breaking research on stopping light—a crucial step in developing memory for quantum computing for the next generation of computers.'

'What?' I stared at her blankly.

'Haha, that's exactly how he responded,' Kavya said gleefully. 'I told him I wanted to do research and come up with experiments of my own to further stop light for longer durations, by storing a single photon using a much larger silicate crystal. He was completely zapped!'

We looked at each other and almost split our sides laughing. Lyka jumped around, not knowing how else to respond.

'I got to sit on a bike after so long! It was a-maz-ing! The fresh strong wind blowing, the beautiful scenery all around . . . wow! And then we rode up and down the slopes of the hilly area near Khadakvasla Lake . . . it was just . . .

mesmerizing!' Kavya held Lyka's head and gazed into her eyes, as if talking to her.

'Hmm . . . someone has a major crush,' I teased her.

'You know, we sat on the banks of the lake for a long time, sipping hot chai and eating corn. The huge lake went all the way to the foot of the hills that envelop the city, and they were so green and their peaks were covered by clouds! And there were a few boats in the lake and some kids playing on the bank and . . . It was picture perfect!' Kavya went on in a rush.

'Adi has turned you into a poet, Kuhu. By the way, did you hear what I just said?'

She sighed. 'Yes, madam, I did. But it's funny—he's a gem of a guy, yet surprisingly, the more time I spend with him, the more I see him only as a good friend, that's all. At first I had a major crush on him but now I don't feel like flirting with him; I don't feel attracted towards him in any way! Isn't that a bit weird?'

She paused, and we both watched Lyka sniff at something on the road.

'I mean, just think about it. He's probably the nicest guy I have ever met, and all I see in him is a great friend who makes me laugh, who I'm comfortable with. You know what, Pihu, I like it that way. I don't have to do anything to impress him, I can just be myself. With him, I just feel normal, comfortable and peaceful.'

'Now that's a mature Kavya I never knew existed!'

Kavya giggled. 'Yeah, I don't know what has happened to me. I just hope I am not losing my touch. There are so many guys in Pune that I am yet to flirt with!'

We walked in silence around the quiet park, lit by the magical moonlight. An old couple sat on a bench, talking softly. Some kids played on the grass while their parents took a lazy post-dinner stroll. A boy had set up his telescope and was gazing through it at the starry sky. Everything was so serene, so peaceful.

I smiled at Kavya and after a minute of silence, started humming an old Hindi song.

'Thandi hawa, ye chandni suhaani . . .'

Kavya hummed along.

'Ae mere dil, suna koi kahani . . .'

7

Reaching for the skies

Next morning, we quickly got ready and were out of the house in half an hour, picking up Sakshi on the way. As promised, Adi was going to show us around the airbase, and we were all looking forward to it. I was eager to see just what it was that had fascinated Bhaiya so much, while Kavya, I suspected, just wanted more of Adi's company.

As we approached our destination, our thoughts were interrupted by the most ear-shattering noise we had ever heard. We immediately popped our heads out of the autorickshaw and what we saw left us speechless for the next few seconds. Metres above our head flew the most powerful and advanced flying machine that the Indian Air Force boasted of—the Sukhoi-30 MKI fighter jet! Dark grey in colour, twin-tailed with a large wingspan and proudly displaying the tri-coloured IAF symbol, the fighter looked mean and handsome at the same time—much more impressive than in the pictures that Bhaiya had shown me once. But it flew past us so fast, by the time we could react, it was long gone, vanishing into the grey clouds dotting the blue sky.

'Wow!' I exclaimed, the noise still ringing in my ears. 'Did you see that? I mean, I've seen these things on TV and in films, but this was . . .' I couldn't find words to describe the experience.

'It's like that scene in *Rang De Basanti*,' replied an equally-awestruck Kavya. 'You know, where those guys go to those open fields and jump at the jet that takes off right above their heads?'

I had already started to get an idea about why Bhaiya was so crazy about the IAF, but decided to reserve my judgment till the end of the day.

Adi's home was a big, beautiful bungalow with a lush garden at the entrance. In the veranda stood a wooden swing, surrounded on three sides by plants. A wind chime tinkled at the door, breaking the serene silence.

After introducing us to his parents, Adi announced, 'Let's leave for the Family Day right now. We are already late.'

'What is this Family Day?' I enquired.

'It's the first step to show you that IAF is not just a *job*,' he retorted. Ah, he had still not forgotten my offhand remark.

His dad clarified, 'One Sunday every month, the airbase is opened up for family members to visit and explore.'

My heart was racing as we got into Air Commodore Prabhakar's sky-blue official Maruti Gypsy. We took a round of the entire office area, bathed in greenery, before finally stopping at the runway near the air traffic control tower. From there, we could see five Sukhois lined up next to each other, their cockpits open, with people standing on the ladder and peeping inside. After checking out the ATC tower, we made our way to the aircraft.

I stood in front of a jet, admiring its sheer size. It looked bigger, more dominating and much more handsome than what I had seen in the air sometime back. The sun reflected off its shining surface, as if surrendering in its attempt to penetrate the mighty machine. The sight of not one but five such jets standing together was truly captivating, and I kept staring open-mouthed for a few minutes.

'You have to see them to believe them, isn't it?' Adi remarked as he signalled to me to climb into the cockpit.

Inside the cockpit, all I could see was a large panel full of meters, electronic displays and buttons of different sizes. In that seat, I felt a sense of power and authority, envisaging myself ruling the skies, joystick in hand. The mere thought of flying this super-expensive and super-advanced fighter with the responsibility of protecting my country gave me goosebumps. The more fascinated I got, the sadder I started to feel for Bhaiya. It pained me to realize that he had had to give up the thrill and exhilaration that came with flying and conquering the vast skies.

'Come on Payal, let's go. Are you planning to fly off in that thing?' Adi knocked on the cockpit to get me out of my trance.

Back at Adi's home, we found ourselves chatting at the lunch table. I could now appreciate Bhaiya's and Adi's attachment to flying, but still had a few doubts in my mind.

'Adi, isn't it tough to keep shifting from one city to another every three–four years?' I asked.

'Well, it is initially,' he replied after a pause. 'But slowly, you get used to it. And then you start loving it, like I do. One, you get to see so many new towns, explore the country. Two, you meet so many people and make new friends. Three, you learn to adapt yourself well to any environment.'

I was still not convinced. 'But what about the fact that you risk your life fighting on the border or flying those crazily-fast jets? And, god forbid, what happens when there is a war?'

'Soldiers die so that the country can sleep in peace—if that doesn't give you an adrenaline rush, I don't know what else will. The thrill of serving your nation, the pride of wearing that uniform, not to mention a lively social life with every facility you need at your fingertips—what more can you ask for?'

Kavya, busy munching till now, took a break from eating and asked, 'Then why are you studying English literature instead of flying that Sukhoi thing?'

Adi's tone immediately changed. 'I failed the medical test. My vision was not perfect and my heart had some kind of murmur.'

The bitterness in his voice was hard to miss.

As the sun set, we went out for a walk around the campus and soon reached the sports complex. Both Sakshi's and my eyes lit up, even as Kavya cried out, 'Oh no, we are not going there, please! That's all we do every day!'

But the two of us were already heading towards the badminton court, led by Adi.

Two good-looking young officers were already there, knocking around. Kavya's eyes lit up and even I found them extremely watchable. One of them asked Adi, 'You guys want to join?'

'Not me, but my friends here would definitely want to,' Adi replied, gesturing towards me and Sakshi.

One of them smiled and waved at me. 'Why don't you come on my side, so that we can even the teams out?'

I wasn't sure what to do. Sakshi, as usual, came to my rescue and replied politely, 'Well, actually, we would like to be together in one team, if you don't mind.'

The officer raised an eyebrow at Adi, who whispered to us, 'Hey, I understand you girls play well. But these two are the Command champions and are training to break into the IAF team. It might be better for you to team up with one of them each.'

'We will see. Can we get on with the game now?' Sakshi smiled calmly.

I adored Sakshi's self-confidence and was determined to learn at least that from her, if nothing else.

This was the first time we were playing doubles as a team, and it was another ball game altogether. The dynamics, the strategy, the skill—everything was completely different. It was all about the rhythm between the teammates.

But as we played together that evening, something clicked. The chemistry, the understanding, the synchrony—we were like a well-oiled machine. We called for our shots in time, covered for each other on the court and coordinated the smashes and drops.

To their dismay, the potential IAF badminton team lost to two novice girls that evening without giving much of a fight. To say that they were stunned would be an understatement.

Sakshi and I high-fived after the game.

'You are a magician!' I shouted and hugged her.

'*We,*' Sakshi corrected.

★ ★ ★

After we went back to Adi's home, he gave Kavya a small gift. 'To celebrate our newfound friendship. I hope it lasts forever.'

Kavya tore open the wrapping to find a cute brown toy Labrador, sitting on a colourful mat in a wooden basket, with two little pups trying to peeping out. Her face flushed with pleasure.

'She is *my* Lyka!' Kavya shouted, hugging Adi and placing the memento carefully in her handbag. 'Adi, this is the best present ever!'

We thanked Adi's parents and were off in an auto, downgraded from the supersonic king of the skies to the sputtering servant of the roads.

Once we were home, I quickly finished my dinner and gave Bhaiya a call.

'Bhaiya, why did you capitulate?' I came to the point instantly. 'I went to the air force station in Pune today. It was awesome! For one day, I lived the life that you wanted. I could feel your passion. And it hurt me to think that you gave it all up . . .'

Bhaiya sighed. 'Payal, do we need to walk down that road again? I thought we were done with that discussion.'

Hearing the pain in his voice, I calmed down and said, 'I just wish everyone in this world could follow their passion.'

'That can only happen in an ideal world. Look, I used to wish the sky was mine, but I have lived through that pain and gotten over it. Can I change the past now? No. So I have closed that chapter of my life and moved on.'

'But I don't want to make compromises with my life, Bhaiya,' I said in a low voice.

'You will not, my stupid girl. I'll make sure you don't, I promise. Now, cheer up and tell me, what else have you been doing in Pune?'

We chatted for another half an hour. A little while after we had hung up Vishakha Bhabhi called.

'Your brother is worried about you. He said that your head is full of so many questions and thoughts that you may over-complicate your life.' However, she didn't sound perturbed at all.

'And what was your reply?'

She laughed.

'Your family has a worry bug! I told him you are at a crossroads in your life, and you need to sort things out by yourself. We should let you go through this experience without interfering—it's an essential part of your growing up and you will certainly come out stronger.'

After talking to Bhabhi, I felt liberated. I was sure her words would have soothed Bhaiya a little as well.

It's funny how, no matter how strong we are, we always end up looking for reassurances from our loved ones. I from Bhaiya, Bhaiya from Bhabhi . . . we are all vulnerable inside, I guess.

8

The turning point

The next few weeks were quite tough for me on the court, but extremely enjoyable at the same time, given my activities outside the camp.

'The four corners, that's all there is to the opponent's court,' Purab told me during a gruelling coaching session, after one of my shots got killed by a return smash. 'No matter how fast your smash is, or how neat your drop near the net is—if it's not near any of those corners, it's an absolute waste of your energy.'

I had always implemented this advice instinctively in my game thus far, but now I was being forced to use this as a conscious weapon.

'I don't want to see any of your smashes falling in the middle of the court, understand?' Purab's loud voice continued to echo around the court as I sweated. 'The more you focus on the side gallery, girl, the more in control of the rally you will be. A shuttle is useful only if it kisses the lines, always remember that!'

I couldn't help but smile at Purab's expression 'kiss the lines'. I inscribed the phrase in my head.

During the afternoon session that day, Sakshi and I approached Purab, who was busy jotting down notes on his pad.

Sakshi spoke up, 'Purab, we want to play doubles together. I think we make a good team.'

Purab was silent for a while as he stared at his notes. Finally he said, 'All right, if that's what you both want, then so be it. But remember, it will only be harder for you. By no means will I let you compromise your efforts on your singles games.'

Life off the court, however, was more relaxed than I could have imagined. Kavya and I were having the time of our lives—no restrictions from parents, shopping at the coolest spots in the city, relishing the local delicacies, watching loads of movies and making frequent trips to scenic spots outside Pune.

Kavya and Adi's friendship had grown from strength to strength in a very short time. They spent many evenings together. Neither of them ever mentioned anything about taking their relationship one step further, though. Sometimes I wondered why, because they seemed perfect for each other.

Sakshi and I, too, shared a great rapport, thanks to the extended time we spent with each other on court. We understood each other well, and empathized with the other's aspirations and motivations. We were quite similar in nature, besides, of course, the common thread of badminton that bonded us together.

For some reason, though, Kavya and Sakshi didn't get along very well. Not that they had ever had a fight or even an argument, but there was this invisible wall that seemed to force them to keep a distance. In fact, Sakshi often tried to be friendlier, but Kavya never reciprocated. This was strange, because usually she was extremely friendly and outgoing, more so than me.

A week before the camp was to close, we were all sitting at the McDonalds on J.M. Road. Kavya finished eating before any of us. She got up, saying, 'God, you guys eat so slowly! I'm going to Crossword to grab a magazine.'

'I'm done too; I will join you. I need to catch the special report on Chinese badminton in the latest *Sportstar*.' Sakshi made another attempt at breaking the ice.

As Adi watched Kavya leave, the look in his eyes made me uneasy. I decided to keep mum, though.

My qualms came true when he murmured, 'I think I am falling for her.'

'Excuse me?'

He looked up at me and smiled.

'Is there anything wrong in that? She has already become my best friend, and we click so well.'

I remembered the debate I'd had with Kavya back in Lucknow a few months back. I had been of the firm opinion that a boy and a girl can never remain just friends and are bound to get romantically attached, sooner or later. Kavya had brushed aside the theory with contempt. And then we had laughed about how we had sounded like scriptwriters of a typical Bollywood love story!

'Payal, what do you think? Should I tell her?'

I was brought back to the present by Adi's fingers tapping my hand. I looked at him intently and replied, 'Hmm . . . Adi, I don't know. I mean, you are a great guy, don't get me wrong. It's just that I know Kavya like no one else, and she is currently not in a frame of mind to enter a relationship.'

'You don't *get* into a frame of mind to enter a relationship, Payal. It just happens. I may sound clichéd, but that's how it is.'

I so wanted to change the topic.

'I have no right to interfere. So do what you think is correct, Adi. But if I were you, I would never let anything spoil the friendship that you two share right now.'

I knew Kavya did not see Adi in the same light as he did her, but she also didn't want a nice guy like him to get hurt. I just hoped he had got the hint.

We drank our shakes in an awkward silence, and I started wondering if I had said more than I should have. My misery was cut short by the return of the other two.

Kavya winked at Adi and said, 'I got the latest research journal on quantum computing.' She burst out laughing and so did he, much to my relief. That's the magic of this girl, I thought. No wonder he's got feelings for her.

★ ★ ★

It was the last week of the camp. Everyone was focused on the final matches. Each player in the group was scheduled to play the other in a marathon session lasting the entire week. As expected, Sakshi was steamrolling her opponents with ease, not having dropped even a single game in any of her matches.

But for me, the biggest revelation had been the enormous measures by which my game had improved. It was heartening to see that the effort and dedication I had put in during my training was doing wonders to my game now. I was finally at peace with myself, ready to go back home and battle life again with full gusto.

Just one small hitch, though. My final game was against Sakshi.

This was the last game of the camp, and all the other players had gathered to watch the battle. They had previously fallen victim to Sakshi's prowess on court and I was the only one who had not played against her yet. As a doubles team, Sakshi and I had been nicknamed 'The Unstoppables', and there was an ongoing debate as to who was the better player. Hence, this final clash was a moment everyone had been waiting for.

I started out slowly as usual, and was down 1–5 within no time. But I was not as nervous and confused as usual, and I believed I could fight back. My game started to come together gradually, and I had reduced the lead to 9–11 by the time we reached the midway mark. I was beginning to match Sakshi shot by shot, picking up her smashes with comfort and nullifying her incessant attack with some well-timed drops. We got on level terms very quickly and at 18–18, the excitement got the better of the audience, who started shouting for us. However, Sakshi never got flustered and kept up her attack to break the defensive barrier I had set up. Her persistence was rewarded when two supersonic smashes down the line sealed the game for her at 21–19.

As I took a break to moisten my parched throat, I felt supremely confident. Even though I had lost the game by a narrow margin, I knew that I had already shocked Sakshi with my ability to match her aggression. For the first time, I actually believed that I could beat the champion of the camp.

When the second game started, there was a new swiftness in my steps. My strength was my strong net play and I employed that to perfection, making Sakshi scramble on the court. *Kiss the lines*, I kept reminding myself. For the first time, I led Sakshi, comfortably up 11–7 at midway. And then, as if boosted by an adrenaline shot, I changed my game tactics from smart net play and precise placements to exploding smashes and aggressive shot selection. I was surprised by my ability to play with such hostility. I hadn't known that my arms were capable of producing those powerful smashes I had always admired Sakshi for.

I was now jumping in the air to smash from the baseline—an issue on which Purab had spent hours working with me. Sakshi was taken aback and by the time she could adjust to the new me, I had wrapped up the game 21–11.

This was the first time in two months that Sakshi had lost a game. I had shocked not only myself, but the entire audience. I could see sheer delight written all over Purab's face.

None of the coaches came to give us any advice during the break. Later, Purab told us that he had wanted us to fend for ourselves; this was proving to be a great test of our mental strength.

When the final game started, both of us knew that the battle had now boiled down to physical and mental strength, rather than badminton skills. We started off cautiously, trying to ensure we didn't commit any unforced errors. If the first two games were about ruthless attack and acute angles, then this one was more about long rallies and watchful placements.

Being familiar with Sakshi's strengths and weaknesses, I was playing mental games now, trying to outwit her with trick shots. But she kept her calm and proceeded with a simple game plan. She knew I was not capable of the aggression I had shown in the last game, simply because my body would not support me. She purposely engaged me in long rallies and played along without trying to kill the shuttle. As expected, I slowly started to wear down as each point stretched longer and my arms started to tire. This was exactly what Sakshi had been waiting for. The moment one of my returns would get weak and slow, she would jump gleefully in the air and smash the shuttle hard down the line, way out of my reach.

As Sakshi expanded her lead to 14–10, I decided to cut back the long rallies and drop the shuttle earlier, only to save some energy. But that did not work either, as Sakshi had anticipated this, and was quick to reach all those delicate drops that had made me so lethal thus far. The haste to end points soon also made me commit more unforced errors than before.

Even as I tried to improve my footwork and placements, it was not enough to stop the momentum Sakshi had gained. I kept within possible reach of a lead, but Sakshi ensured it never threatened her, as the score transformed from 16–13 to 18–15 to 20–17. Sakshi was now controlling the game well, and we both knew it was my lack of fitness and strength that had proved to be the differentiator in an otherwise equally matched game.

As Sakshi hit the final shot of the match on the back-gallery corner, on my backhand, my tired legs were just not swift enough any more to reach out for it, and the epic match finally came to an end.

Overwhelmed with emotions and exhausted, the two of us simply sat on the court, trying to get our breath back. Finally we got up and hugged each other.

Purab came up to us, looking ecstatic.

'This camp is in its tenth year, and I doubt that it has ever seen the quality of badminton it witnessed today. You two were like warriors!'

Just then, I saw Kavya standing at a little distance. For a few seconds, she looked angry and hurt, as if something was pinching her inside. But she smiled when she saw me looking at her, and sat down with us, showering praises on our game.

The final day of the camp was more of a formality, with no actual training taking place. All the coaches gave individual feedback to each player and discussed any specific concerns. As everyone was bidding goodbye, Purab clapped his hands loudly for the last time.

'The last two months have been fascinating,' he began. 'I witnessed some spectacular badminton, honest commitment, a willingness to succeed and above all, such passion! I saw you people learning with enthusiasm and enjoying yourselves on court. I saw you guys sweating for hours and playing like there's no tomorrow. But the one thing that was common in everyone's eyes was the love for this beautiful game. THAT is what makes this camp a success.'

He paused as everyone cheered and clapped.

'Wherever you are and whatever you do, no matter how old you may get and how busy your schedule may be—never turn your back on the game; keep playing—play for fun, play to win, play to relive past memories, play to relieve your stress—whatever your reason may be, never stray too far from that court. I promise you, it will always bring a smile on your face. God bless you all, thank you.'

Claps thundered across the stadium and Purab was soon surrounded by a group of pupils, wanting to thank him individually.

Back home, as Kavya picked up Adi's gift from her bedside table to pack it in her suitcase, Lyka started to bark, tugging at her trousers and jumping to get hold of the gift.

'Not again, Lyka.' Kavya patted her. 'Pihu, doesn't she look so cute when she does this?'

Lyka did not like the showpiece; she felt jealous that there was another dog in the house whom Kavya seemed to love more.

I didn't respond to Kavya's comment and went up to the window, staring out at the horizon, the cool evening breeze playing with my hair.

'Miss Pihu, which world are you in? In fact, you have been very quiet all day today, what's up? I bet you didn't even thank Purab and say goodbye to him.'

Not knowing how to tell her about the epiphany I'd had, I didn't reply.

'Anyway, let's try to finish packing today itself, so that tomorrow we can spend time with Mausa and Mausiji before leaving for the station.'

'I am not going back,' I said slowly.

Kavya hugged me from behind. 'I know Pihu yaar, even I don't want to go back; this was perhaps the best vacation of my life. I wish it didn't have to end.'

Kavya went back to her packing. I finally turned towards her and said, 'You didn't hear me right, Kuhu. I didn't say "I *don't want* to go back". I am *not* going back.'

Kavya's hands froze as she looked up at me. Confused and dazed, she shouted, 'What?'

I turned back to stare out of the window.

9

Friends fall apart

There was an eerie silence in the room for the next few minutes. Out of the corner of my eye, I saw Lyka quietly slipping out. Maybe she had sensed the tension in the air.

I was still at the window. I knew that Kavya was the least of my problems; she was my friend, she would understand. But then I would have to tell Bhaiya, Bhabhi, Mom . . . how would they react? Mom hated badminton; she wanted me to concentrate on academics . . , would I be forced to go the same way as Bhaiya?

'It's high time you stop staring and start talking. Why are you being so dramatic?' Kavya's pitch was loud enough for even the neighbours to hear. I wondered who was actually being more dramatic, but decided not to antagonize my friend further.

I finally moved away from the window, sat down on the bed beside Kavya and held her hand.

'Kuhu, I have given this decision enough thought.'

She became even more baffled.

'I don't think you know what you are talking about!
Either you are on drugs, or you have left your brain behind
on that stupid court of yours!'

I couldn't help laughing.

'Purab called me yesterday and said that I was one of the
best players in the camp. He wants me to train further to
compete for a place in the Pune district team. He also . . .'

'What nonsense, Pihu!' Kavya cut in. 'I mean, I'm happy
that you played so brilliantly and all. But all the others had
come to the camp with the sole purpose of getting into the
district team, because they are all professionals. You didn't
join this camp for that!'

'I know, Kuhu. But that's what I want to tell you. It's
not just about staying back for the district team selection.
It's beyond that. I . . .'

She was in no mood to listen. 'And what about your
results? You do remember your entrance results are going
to be out shortly, right?'

'Will you even let me speak? And please calm down!'

'Calm down my foot! *I* brought you to Pune and it's my
responsibility to get you back home safely. I'm calling up
Bhaiya; maybe he can get some sense into your head.'

Before I could react, she had already dialled Bhaiya and
given him a quick update. She handed over the phone to
me, her face red with excitement.

I spoke as composedly as I could. 'Hi Bhaiya. You can either
start scolding me, just like this best friend of mine did, or you
can first listen to me patiently and then say what you like.'

The answer was evident to both of us. 'You're on speaker
phone, Payal. Mom's also here,' Bhaiya told me.

I took a deep breath and started, 'Okay, you remember

the discussion we had had that evening at home, right? I have been living in fear, a fear that I would have to live my life doing what everyone wanted or expected me to do. What rankled most was that even though I knew I wanted to follow my passion, I hadn't found it! You had asked me to search my soul deeper to find an answer to that question, remember? I think this trip came at the right time, because it is helping me do just that.'

There was no response from the other end.

'I've always loved badminton, you know that. But this camp has made me realize that I am actually extremely good at it. This is it! I saw the potential inside me and trust me, it will amaze you as well.'

I could hear Mom sigh.

'It only struck me when the camp got over that this was it! I never want to leave the court. Nothing gives me more peace and happiness than being there. And to top it all, God has given me the talent to back up this love. Please Bhaiya, Mom, this is where I want to be, this is what I want to do.'

'But have you thought about the practicalities? Your studies, your family, your friends . . . are you ready to give up everything for a passion that you are still in the process of discovering?' Kavya could not resist any longer and spoke loudly enough for everyone to hear.

'If it doesn't need sacrifice, then it's not really a passion, is it?' I countered.

'So what's the deal?' Bhaiya enquired finally.

'I will be training for the district team, the selections for which will happen after a month. If selected, I will play in the Maharashtra senior state selection tournaments, three in all, in which I will compete against other district team players. At the end of those, depending on the points that I have collected based on my performances, I may be selected to the state team. Once in the state team for the year, I will play major national tournaments, gather points and . . .'

'Payal, do you realize that all these are *professional* tournaments with *professional* players? Are you even going to fit in? I hope you know that things don't happen in real life like they do in movies—Adi told me that players take years to play juniors, establish themselves and then finally end their careers without even reaching the state level! You think you can bypass all that and become a national player within one year?' Kavya's ire was rising by the minute. I wondered why she was getting so bothered.

'You are absolutely right. I don't know if I can match their calibre. But at least I will not regret that I didn't try.'

'But are you prepared to lose one academic year?' Bhaiya asked.

'Thousands of kids in this country do that for some reason or the other. And in this case, I get to do what I love doing, rather than learning to love what I do.' I was reminded of my conversation with that guy on the train.

'And where are you going to live?'

'Initially, I will stay in Pune with my friend Sakshi. After that, Purab, our coach, will arrange accommodation for us according to where the camps will be held; I don't know in which city . . .' The line suddenly got disconnected.

It was only after half an hour that Bhaiya called back to give me some good news. Mom had reluctantly agreed to my wish. Surprisingly, she had listened quietly to the whole conversation between Bhaiya and me earlier too. Maybe she had understood that this time, I had actually found my calling in life.

I was ecstatic. 'Thank you! I love you both so much! You are my strength and I promise I will never let you down.'

However, Kavya's face still had disapproval written all over.

'Why are you so disturbed by my decision, Kuhu? Even Bhaiya and Mom are convinced now.'

'I think it's foolish. What's wrong with you, Pihu? I am the one known to take rash and crazy decisions, not you. You were so level-headed, but now I am afraid you have lost your mind somewhere on that court!'

'What exactly is the problem?' I knew I would never be completely comfortable with my plan if my best friend didn't approve of it.

'Let's not go into all that. I have a lot of packing to do.' I had never found Kavya so cold. 'Let's just say that I wish you all the best for your newfound "passion", your new life and your new friends!'

I sensed something was wrong. Was it really the badminton that was troubling Kavya or something else? But before I could probe any further, she was out of the room.

★ ★ ★

As we moved our luggage out of the house that Sunday evening, Lyka sat crouched under the table in the drawing room, looking at us with gloomy eyes. Kavya pulled her out. Lyka looked longingly as Kavya hugged her and struggled hard not to cry.

Adi and Sakshi were already at the station by the time we reached there. Adi got busy settling Kavya's luggage while she stood on the platform, morose, sipping the hot tea I had got for us from a nearby vendor.

'I'll miss my bubbly friend,' I remarked.

'You won't need her any more. You have new friends now!' Kavya sneered, with a glance towards Sakshi.

'Oh, so this is what that was all about!' I exclaimed. 'Don't be silly, Kuhu. I would have taken this decision even if Sakshi was not there. This has nothing to do with her.'

Kavya drank her tea in silence.

'Kuhu, I will not be able to do this on my own if my best friend does not support me.'

'You don't need anyone's support now. You are a free bird,' she responded dryly as she moved towards her uncle to bid him goodbye.

I felt angry, sad and disappointed at the same time. Why was she making me feel as if I was sacrificing my friendship with her to achieve my dreams? Why couldn't she grow up?

My chain of thoughts snapped when my eyes met Adi's. I could see the pain that he was desperately trying to hide. He tried to smile at me but failed miserably. A wave of guilt flooded my heart. Had I made a mistake? What if Kuhu also liked him and they had not confessed this to each other only because of me? Would Kuhu hate me even more if I told her?

As I saw Kavya give Adi a final goodbye hug, I trembled. For a moment, I thought of telling Kavya everything, but I guess Adi read my mind and shook his head, looking into my eyes.

The engine whistled; Kavya came up to me and held my hand.

'All the best,' she said formally. 'May god be with you.'

I wanted to hug her tight, to tell her how much I was going to miss her and how incomplete my life would be without her cheerful and inspiring presence. But before I could even come close to her, she had climbed into the train, which slowly started to roll out.

Kavya waved to everyone, and I felt a sharp spasm of pain, guilt and sadness cloud my heart. My mind was numb and my eyes were full of tears, which were now overflowing on to my cheeks. I suddenly felt so lonely that I wanted to climb on to the train and go back to the comfort of home and the company of my best friend.

As I stood there on the platform, watching the last bogey move out of the station through tear-filled eyes, I felt weak, tired and lonely.

'Have I sacrificed too much to run after my dreams?' I asked myself as glimpses of home flashed in my mind. I saw Bhabhi and me laughing together, I saw Kavya pulling me into a shop on one of our shopping excursions, I saw my former teachers laughing at my foolish decision, I saw Sakshi holding my hand, pulling me away from Kavya . . . Feeling overwhelmed, I sat on a nearby bench, threw my head back and closed my eyes.

I had never felt this disturbed before.

10

A silent bond

The cool and tranquil night breeze in Pune is one of the key reasons why it's so great to live there. It relaxes and invigorates your mind at the same time. No wonder there were so many people in the park on J.M. Road that beautiful moonlit night.

The two of us also sat on the grass, the therapeutic breeze working its magic on us.

After a short while Sakshi finally said, 'So how are you feeling?'

My gaze shifted from the sparkling stars in the sky to the grass on the ground.

'I don't know,' I said after a long pause. 'There are too many thoughts crowding my mind . . .'

'I can understand how tough it must be for you, Payal, to take such a bold step. But I am so proud of you! You did the right thing, and you'll realize that in time.'

'I see that my psychologist is back in action,' I smiled.

'Call me whatever you want, but all I try to do is clear your mind so that you can think straight. Emotions cloud one's thinking, Payal. They do you no good, especially in times like these, where being courageous and determined is not only a necessity, but a life saver.'

I felt better. But the thought of my best friend sitting in a train hundreds of miles away, seething with jealousy, was a dampener.

'Have I lost Kuhu because of her foolishness?' I wondered.

★ ★ ★

'You made a sensible decision. Good.' Purab wore a warm smile the next morning at the stadium as he welcomed me.

As I greeted him, Purab's expression changed suddenly to his usual focused and stern one.

'Do you know why you lost to your friend the other day, despite winning the second game in the most scintillating manner you have ever played?' he asked.

'Fitness and strength, right?'

'Well, that solves half the problem. At least you know what you need to do!'

I grinned at him.

He led me to the gym next to the stadium, while Sakshi headed towards Court No.1 for a practice session.

'Your superb natural talent takes you to a level far beyond your years,' Purab continued. 'But your lack of fitness and strength brings you right back on the ground. All I am trying to do is to make you fly to that level again . . . fly strong and fly long. Don't you want to?'

My cheeks flushed. 'I am ready, Purab,' I said with full enthusiasm.

I had not run as much in all my eighteen years as I did in those few weeks. I spent countless hours on the weights and machines under the strict guidance of a professional trainer, and was forced to continue till I felt my limbs would drop off from sheer stress. My wrists and shoulders, in particular, were put through tremendous strain, to make them capable of killing the shuttle. Customized exercises were designed for my calf muscles, to make them strong enough to carry my body swiftly for three continuous sets of a match. During the initial days, I would be so dead after a three-hour stint in the gym that I would have no energy on the court.

'Jump higher! You need to meet the shuttle much earlier,' Purab shouted during an extended practice session one day, meant to fine-tune my smashes and test whether my arm could take the strain for long durations. Purab was very clear that the only way I could be a real threat to top players was by complementing my net play with aggressive smashes and long rallies—something I hoped the extensive focus on physical fitness would help me achieve.

It was turning out to be a gritty test of my strength and fitness. The entire court was flooded with shuttles, so much so that all one could see was a layer of white covering the wood. Amidst the sea of shuttles stood Purab and I, both on the same side of the court. Purab tossed a shuttle up in the air for me to jump and smash. 'Hit!' he shouted. Seconds after my feet landed back, another shuttle was popped up for me to smash. 'Hit!' he shouted again. And again another shuttle, another cry . . . and so it continued endlessly! Every time my smashes weakened, Purab would roar, 'Kill it, dammit! Is that all you've got? Is this why you stayed back in Pune? Don't waste my time if you can't kill that shuttle!'

The exercise continued until I dropped down on the

court, dead tired. Purab sat down beside me, surrounded by pristine white feathers all around.

'Kiss the lines; forget this rule at your own peril, girl!' he said. After a short discussion, he went off to check on the other players.

Sakshi joined me a little later and sat down on the steps.

'So champ, I guess those agonizing hours in the gym are paying off now!'

I smiled at her. 'Earlier I would rarely smash, banking mostly on my drops. But now, I am not afraid to hit—to hit strong and hit long.'

'Excellent! So, to celebrate your newfound confidence, I have tomorrow all planned out for us.'

'What do you mean? What about practice?'

'The coaches are giving all of us a day off tomorrow—kind of a break to recharge our batteries, before the final burst of practice until the selections.'

'Hmm . . . And what do you have in store for us?'

'We will get up early in the morning to go for a long run around the park . . .'

'Ah, what an exciting start to a holiday. You are so much fun, Sakshi,' I teased.

Sakshi looked so sad that I burst out laughing.

'I'm sorry, just kidding. Please continue.'

'After that, a nice south Indian breakfast at Vaishali, along with their trademark aromatic filter coffee.'

I was now getting interested. A leisurely south Indian breakfast early in the morning at a happening joint, after a tiring but refreshing run, sounded like a good change from the monotony of the bread and eggs breakfast at the guest house. Moreover, the idea of going back to Vaishali, the place where Adi had taken all of us the very first day, sounded nice—if for nothing else, then at least for bringing back fond memories of the time when all was hunky-dory between Kavya and me.

Sakshi continued, breaking my chain of thoughts. 'After that, we come back and change and head out for a shopping extravaganza—the fashion street-heavy bargaining-cheap jewellery-Osho chappals type! I mean, we have been here for so long and haven't shopped the way real Pune girls do, isn't it?'

I loved the idea.

'And finally, we wrap up the day by gorging on some spicy Thai food and then treating ourselves to the yummy Naturals ice cream at Koregaon Park!'

I gave her a thumbs up as we parted to resume our training for the day.

My mind was not on the game as I went through the drills. I knew Sakshi was doing all this only to cheer me up and try to compensate for Kavya's absence. I was still angry with Kavya, but a small part of me craved for her company and support, without which I felt incomplete.

'I will call her tonight. It's been so long,' I said to myself as I smashed hard down the line, the feathers of the shuttle blissfully kissing the sidelines of the court to perfection.

That night, I stood on the balcony of the guest house, gazing at the twinkling stars. With buoyant optimism, I dialled Kavya's mobile number. It was switched off, so I tried her landline. Her father picked up.

'Hi Uncle. How are you?' I asked.

'Oh wow, Payal beta? It's been so long, how are you?'

'I am fine, Uncle. Is Kuhu there?'

'Just hold on beta, let me check,' he said. I heard him call out, 'Kavya! Pihu's called. Come fast!'

Then I heard her high-pitched voice in the background, 'Tell her I am not at home!'

There was an awkward pause, after which her father replied, 'Beta, I think Kavya is out with some friends. I will ask her to call you once she's back.'

I sighed. 'Uncle, tell her she can't fool me. I simply wanted her to know that I stayed back for the game and nothing else, that's all. The moment she understands this and stops behaving like a kid, she can call me back. Good night, take care,' I ended the conversation in a tone laced with both dejection and anger.

★ ★ ★

We spent the last few days before the selections perfecting our game without putting our bodies through too much stress. Sakshi and I were made to work more on our backhand, which Purab felt was still not potent enough. Purab also made us watch videos of world champions' matches. From Susi Susanti to Camilla Martin to Xie Xingfang, we watched all the famous matches and in every match we tried to analyze the dos and don'ts that could take our own game to the next level.

A day before the selections were to begin, Purab came up to me and said, 'Payal, I know this has been an unexpected journey for you. Let me tell you one secret, young lady. If I had to place my money on someone from this camp making it big, it would be you.

'Yes, I will pick you ahead of Sakshi,' he continued, noticing the surprise on my face. 'Sakshi is more experienced, agreed, and hence more confident and stable in her game. But the past month has drastically changed the way you approach your game. You are turning out to be the perfect all-rounder that I have always envisaged.'

My heart was racing.

'Don't get too excited, though. The one thing that can come in the way of you achieving your true potential is your mental make-up. Nervousness is your biggest enemy; the sooner you can defeat it and settle down in your game, the higher will be your chances of defeating even the best in the business.'

That night, I called up home.

'It's the first big test of my life, Bhaiya. I mean, it's a huge stage and almost everyone there is going to be a professional player. And then I will be there—a girl who started playing badminton seriously only a few months back!'

'Payal, I wish I was there, more than anything else. But I am so caught up at office that it will take me another couple of weeks to sort things out. But I promise I will be there with you at your next tournament!'

Before I could hit the bed, the doorbell rang. I answered and was surprised to see a couriered package in my name.

Upon opening it, I found the latest Yonex Carbonex-30 Muscle racquet, weighing a mere 85 g, sleek and shining in metallic black. Attached to it was a small note in Bhaiya's writing:

In all your troubles, in all your worries
In all the times when you see no light.
I'll hold your hand, I'll guide your soul
I'll pray to God that your life shines bright.

All my anxieties vanished in a second. I knew that somehow or the other, he would always be there for me.

As I prepared to sleep, I peeped into Sakshi's room to wish her good luck. What I saw shocked me. The normally unemotional Sakshi was standing still, her body resting against the window, her hands holding a picture of her parents, tears rolling down her cheeks. She looked around and saw me at the door.

'I guess I'm not as cool as you thought!' she said in a choked voice. 'I get nervous as well, you know. And when I do, I have no one to talk to except them.' She looked longingly at the picture. 'I just wish they were here . . . to see me, to hold me, to bless me, to . . .' Sakshi burst into tears.

So stunned was I that it took me a moment before I rushed to Sakshi and hugged her.

'I miss them, Payal. I miss them every single day. I am so lonely without them.' She rubbed her eyes.

I didn't know what to say, but simply kept hugging her.

The two of us sat together in silence for a long time.

We may look confident but we all have our fears . . . we may seem independent but we crave for our loved ones . . . we may appear steady but we are emotional at heart.

Sakshi was no different.

11

Pay-off time

It was a bright and sunny morning. I was a bundle of nerves when I got up, despite all the motivating talk the previous day. I shivered at the thought of what lay ahead, and none of my efforts to stay calm seemed to work.

Sakshi, on the other hand, was composed as ever and greeted me with a cheerful smile, her glowing face not showing any trace of her emotions during the previous night. 'PUNE DISTRICT BADMINTON TEAM SELECTION AND RANKING: SENIORS' screamed the heading on the huge notice board below which we stood, alongside numerous other players.

All players had been divided into two groups. The first group consisted of the top sixteen players—the current top eight district players, top four university players and top four players from the official inter-corporate tournament. The other group, our group, consisted of 128 qualifiers, divided into sixteen pools of eight each.

In the qualifying round, sixteen players were to be selected in a knockout format. After that, in the main draw, these qualifiers would compete with the top sixteen players.

The top four players making it to the semi-finals would automatically qualify for the district team, with the other four players being selected by the selectors, based on their overall performance.

'Listen, girls, take one game at a time. And Payal, start slowly, don't be too aggressive or anxious to play your best right at the start. Settle down first, get the rhythm going and then go for your best.'

We headed for the court and as we split up, wished each other good luck.

'If you don't get your smashes right, just continue playing your net game. That's good enough to see you through safely,' Sakshi told me and headed off.

Upon reaching the court, I settled my kit down on my side, took out the beautiful racquet Bhaiya had sent and said a silent prayer. Months of practice, long hours in the gym, Purab's scolding, Sakshi's advice, Kavya's silliness, Bhaiya's encouragement, together with countless moments of tiredness, frustration, ecstasy, confidence, nervousness, uncertainty and courage—everything had boiled down to this moment.

Without prolonging my misery any further, the umpire called for the match to start. My nervousness poked its ugly head out early on, as I mistimed my shots and my feet moved reluctantly. Paying no heed to Purab's advice, I tried to hit my way out of the anxiety, going for too much too early on. I only ended up either spraying the shuttle wide off the court or finding the net. The more unforced errors I committed, the more I panicked—I was quickly falling into a vicious cycle—and before I could even realize, I was down 2–10 without my opponent needing to work too hard.

As we took a short water break, I tried my best to calm down. I looked around; there was no Sakshi to bail me out this time. To my dismay, my misery continued even after I got back on the court. Within no time, the game was over, my opponent winning 21–8.

I tried hard to control my tears during the break. I was shivering, thinking that everything could end so soon, in such a humiliating manner. Sitting alone on that court with no support and no spectator, I felt lonely.

Just as I was getting up, my mobile beeped. As soon as I read the message, my heart leapt with joy and my face burst into a smile:

Why is that we hv to lose something to understand its true value? Wish I was thr to hug u n cheer for u. Tell me all abt ur victory after the match. The biggest fool on earth & ur bff—Kuhu

'What timing,' I smiled. I felt I had found the weapon to dispel my fears.

I could feel the rhythm coming back to me. I was gradually getting into the groove and point-by-point, my feet were finding their lost agility, covering the entire court with ease. As I jumped high while returning a serve, my smash echoed through the court and landed right at the corner of the baseline and the backhand sideline—a perfectly sweet spot, way out of the reach of my opponent. I knew I was back in business and though far from my best, managed to wrap up the game 21–10.

During the break, I saw Sakshi and Purab approaching.

'Straight games, no hassles,' was how Purab gleefully

summed up Sakshi's match. But before they could ask me about mine, I was already back on court, not wanting to distract myself from the comfort zone I had entered.

In the final game of that match, right from the word go, I was jumping and hitting hard, my aggression boosted by the confidence in my heart. My net play was nearing its peak, as were my drop shots, all propelling me to a neat victory.

After the game, I called up Kavya without wasting any time.

'You rescued me, girl! Had your message been one minute late, I probably would have been booking my tickets for home right now.'

'I am going to relieve both of us from all the melodrama—where I say sorry and cry, then you accept my apology and cry out of happiness, then we both cry together, thanking god that things are back to their best! So why don't you tell me about your victory now? And about the atmosphere there? And what you did in the past month? And about . . . oh my god, Pihu, do you realize we have so much to catch up on?'

I couldn't have been happier—this was the Kuhu whom I had missed for so long!

Over the next two days, I cruised to victories and qualified for the main draw. Sakshi, too, was as cool as always, effortlessly brushing aside her opponents to qualify for the main draw without any setbacks.

We also played two qualifying matches in the doubles category and our victories there were even more emphatic than in our singles. 'Singles players are never too proficient at the doubles version'—the two of us were debunking this theory in our own style.

'By qualifying for the main draw, you have clearly displayed that you mean business. But the real battle begins from here. These players are experienced professionals, and you will need to play out of your skin to beat them,' Purab told us on the eve of our first match in the main draw.

By the time we won our first two matches, we had managed to grab everyone's attention, from the players to the spectators, from the coaches to the selectors. There was a strong buzz already about the magic of us two debutante girls.

I had never seen as many spectators as there were on the morning of my quarter-finals. As I took out my racquet to get on the court, I asked Purab again in disbelief, 'Are they all here to watch my match?' Along with surprise, there was a sense of sheer joy and belief in myself.

'Yes, just for you! What started as mere ripples have now transpired into a wave of excitement. Those who have already seen you want to check if you are consistent enough to be the "find of the tournament"; those who haven't want to see what the fuss is all about! Either way, Payal, this moment belongs to you.'

I took a deep breath. 'So this is how it feels to be a professional, watched by hundreds.' I was, however, mindful that I should not let all the attention distract me from the game, but never had I been happier. Only one thing bothered me—Neha, my opponent, the current university champion, was left-handed! I had never played against a left-hander before and even though Purab had trained me enough on paper for such an eventuality, I was not very sure how it would translate on court that day.

The loud cheer shifted to an eerie silence as the match

started, the only noise being the thud of the shuttle hitting the taut racquet strings. I had learnt from my mistakes well, and was now content to get my feet moving and exercising my muscles before exploding. However, I was still a bit tentative and found it tough to adjust to Neha's left-handed shots and returns. At the first water break, I was already down 2–7.

Purab came to me and said in a low, calm voice, 'You know, you usually start slowly, so that's okay. There's no need to panic. You are not able to pierce the gaps in her court because you are misreading her.'

I was now walking up and down, wiping my face and flexing my wrists.

It's funny, these coach–player sessions during the breaks. I had watched them so many times on TV and had always found them amusing. The coach would keep on showering encouragement and advice on the players animatedly, doing all the talking and looking straight at his student. I don't even know if the players listened to him at all, because all they would do is drink water, walk up and down, wipe themselves and appear to be in their own world—doing everything other than responding to the coach.

But I listened to Purab carefully. 'So what should I do?' I asked.

'Nothing much. Play as you would normally; just force your mind to interchange the direction of all your shots. Focus your shots more to the left now, to attack her weak backhand.'

Having come this far in the tournament, I was determined not to spoil it all by basic errors in judgment. I absorbed all the pressure and quickly adjusted my game after the break.

The turning point came when, during a long rally, I surprised Neha by jumping high for the first time in the game and smashing hard down the line on her backhand. Neha barely managed to return the shuttle, tumbling on the court in the process. I had already anticipated that the return would be weak and rushed towards the net, jumping again, this time only to kill the shuttle with such thunder that it actually bounced twice on the court before falling dead.

The roar of applause I got for literally pinning the university champion down to the ground was enough to get the adrenaline flowing in my blood.

'Yes!' I pumped my fist and let out a cry of exultation.

After patiently reducing the lead, point by point, and finally overtaking Neha at 11–10, I shifted gears, letting go of the 'patient-long rally-smart drop' game I had been playing till then and allowing my aggression to seize the moment. I started jumping and hitting the shuttle hard more frequently, and moved even quicker on the court to take control of every single point.

Within no time, I stood on a game point. Just then I received a high service from Neha, jumped in my now trademark aggression and smashed hard down Neha's forehand. Neha picked it up well and remained at the back of the court. I jumped again and thundered another smash, this time down the backhand. Neha returned this one as well and stayed back again, as I jumped up a third time to hit hard. However, this time, I changed my mind at the last microsecond while I was airborne, and instead of killing it, dropped the shuttle so deceptively near the forehand corner that Neha remained rooted to the baseline . . . only to surrender the game to me.

During the next game, right from the word go in the next game, I grew so hostile that I incessantly started to smash every single service I faced. My mind was filled with the memory of those long hours on the court with Purab, jumping non-stop and smashing relentlessly till my arms felt as if they were coming out of their sockets. Putting the final nail in the coffin, I shot a cross-court smash from behind my head while airborne and quickly returned to my feet, ready to drop Neha's return with a feather touch near the net. To my surprise, Neha made no move to return that shot—she instead walked towards the net to shake my hand.

The university champion had been destroyed 21–9 on her home turf by a girl who had just trained for a few months!

As I walked to the net, I looked at Purab, pointed to him as a mark of respect and gratitude and remarked gleefully, 'Kissed the lines well, didn't I?'

I was so thrilled that even after leaving the court it took me some time to get my breath back. Only slowly did I start to realize the magnitude of my victory. As unknown people came to congratulate me, it started to sink in.

Slightly anxious, I then quickly went over to my friend's court, fingers crossed.

Far from all this hoopla, Sakshi was quietly but efficiently going around her business of playing exceptional badminton, taking the fourth-ranked district player to task in her trademark style. Bereft of many spectators, with everyone preferring to watch the university champion, we witnessed a perfectly smooth game from the other debutante of the year, as she won without any hiccups 21–7, 21–8. Knowing Sakshi, she was happy to stay away from the limelight, preferring to march towards her aim without any distractions.

Word soon spread about this second consecutive upset of the day, and the officials and team coach gleefully welcomed two new members to the district team.

'It just felt so right, Bhaiya,' I said during my regular phone call to update Bhaiya with all the happenings. 'I can't recollect when I was last so happy and comfortable!'

'So what next?' he asked excitedly.

'You won't believe it! It's the semi-final tomorrow, and guess who I am playing?'

'Well, you and Sakshi have been going great guns so far. You were bound to run into each other sooner or later,' he replied.

'Yeah, but the best part is that since we have already been selected for the district team, the semis and finals are just formalities, only to decide our rankings.'

Neither Sakshi nor I talked about our big clash the next day as we came back home exhausted. We knew we would turn foes on court the next day; the excitement kept us mostly awake on a night that should have ideally given us the most peaceful sleep of our lives.

The stadium was as packed as any of us could have ever imagined. Our game was being billed as the match of the tournament—even when the final was yet to happen! The unbelievable exploits of two young girls from Lucknow had already reached the ears of the who's who of badminton in the city, and almost everyone in Pune who loved to the game was present that day.

The first point itself was one of the longest in the match, Sakshi ending the rally with a powerful smash, leaving me trapped at the other end of the court. But unlike other times, this was not the day for me to start nervously. I was in an aggressive mood and came back strongly on the very next point, controlling the rally throughout, finally catching Sakshi on the wrong foot by dropping the shuttle on her backhand.

The crowd knew right then that they had a game on their hands.

We were hitting hard with all the strength our arms could muster and manage fine with all the finesse our wrists could conjure. Sakshi attacked me incessantly on the backhand, pushing me deeper, trying not to let me control the rallies. But she forgot that my arms were now much stronger than when we had last played. My backhand returns were equally powerful, dispatching the shuttle to Sakshi's back gallery and thus regaining control of the points.

The game see-sawed continuously, and the lead kept exchanging. Sakshi soon realized that she had a battle royale on her hands—I was a different player now and she would need to play her best game to keep me at bay.

The score was 15–15 and we were drenched in sweat. My limbs were strained and my lungs were begging for oxygen. But my mind was working at breakneck speed, trying to devise a new strategy at every point. We were moving up and down the court in a smooth, machine-like rhythm, our racquets in perfect sync with our feet, our minds in tune with our hearts.

But at 19–19, the tension slowly started to mount. Sakshi knew this was her last chance. She realized I was a bit edgy now, given the criticality of the last two points, and decided to keep the rally going for long, waiting for me to commit a mistake. I looked to finish off the point quickly, well aware that the longer the shuttle was in motion, the higher were my chances of making an unforced error.

Sakshi's persistence paid off. She pushed the shuttle accurately to my backhand-baseline corner and I scuttled and returned with shaking wrists. My tentativeness was my undoing. I watched in dismay as the shuttle went wide off the sideline. Sakshi stood at game point at 20–19, and had sensed blood now. As she got ready to serve, it seemed to me that she would send a deep, high serve. My feet unconsciously started to claw back but right before hitting the shuttle, Sakshi held her racquet back and served very short, near the service line. I was taken aback by the deception and, too late to react, was left rooted to the floor. She had narrowly etched out a 21–19 victory!

We stood near the court, panting, then wiped our faces and sipped glucose. The crowd was chanting and clapping in appreciation.

I gave Sakshi a quick glance before heading back, and we exchanged a smile. We knew we were totally enjoying ourselves out there—teasing each other with our badminton skills, challenging each other's strength and stamina, and playing mind games.

In the next game, at first, it seemed as if we resumed from where we had left off. But I quickly realized that Sakshi was having some trouble in picking my cross-court shots because of their angle, and was a bit slow in reaching out to them.

This chink in her armour was enough for me. It gave me control of the points, which I latched on to and thus maintained a steady lead throughout the second game. Sakshi would occasionally crawl back with some amazing net play of her own, but then eventually fall prey to my angles again.

The cycle continued till I was finally on a game point at 20–17, the game still too close for comfort. I had been serving short almost all throughout, changing my tactic from the last game. As I got ready to serve short, I sensed Sakshi was not thinking much about the service; her mind was already racing ahead, strategizing how to answer the cross-court shot. She was leaning forward in anticipation of another short serve. But at the last second, I served the shuttle quick and long, much to Sakshi's surprise, throwing her completely off-balance. She couldn't do much, and watched the shuttle sail past her head helplessly.

I had snatched the second game 21–17!

By the time we started the final game of what was turning out to be an epic battle, our bodies were wilting under the extreme stress and our minds had become numb from the non-stop strategizing over the past two games. It was no longer about skills or talent. It was all going to boil down to physical stamina and mental acuity; and though this had clearly been Sakshi's forte a month back, things were much more even now.

After what seemed like an eternity, we stood at 20–20 for the first time in our fledgling careers. We were battered and bruised; our feet were refusing to move and our lungs refusing to breathe. But our spirits were indomitable, and that's what kept the game alive.

I served high and anticipated Sakshi's return well—a high return on her forehand. With all the courage I could muster, I jumped for a huge kill and then, on a whim, I dropped the shuttle delicately near the net. Sakshi's tired legs were too slow to respond to this and for the first time ever, I scored a match point against her.

At 21–20, the crowd was now wild, and I waited for the noise to subside before embarking on the momentous point. I served short, having no strength left to do otherwise. Sakshi placed the return near the net, no energy left in her either. The shuttle touched the top of the net and nearly stopped in mid-air. I leaped in a last-ditch effort to reach out. The spectators held their breath in anticipation . . . someone let out a squeak . . . time seemed to stand still for a moment.

And then in a flash, it happened—the shuttle danced on top of the net for seconds, failed to cross the net cord and finally fell back on Sakshi's court.

I had stolen the cheekiest of victories I could have ever imagined from the mighty Sakshi!

My mind flashed back to the day I had met Sakshi on the platform. *What a professional player*, I had thought, looking at her racquet. I remembered how much in awe of her I had been the first time I had seen her play. '*Did you play the game in your past life too?*' I had asked her.

And now I had done what I could have never even have dreamt of a few months back—defeated Sakshi 19–21, 21–17, 22–20.

I hugged her—my opponent who had gone from being a friend to a mentor, to a psychologist, to a competitor and now back to being my friend—someone who had been with me all through this journey.

Later that evening, we strategized on the finer aspects of our impending doubles match the next day, which would decide if we got selected for the district team in doubles as well. Sakshi drew an imaginary court on the grass, her two index fingers representing their team.

'When I serve short, Payal, we sometimes leave this area uncovered, and none of us reach it quickly enough,' she was now playing a virtual game with her fingers on the fictitious court over grass. 'If the return comes here, then you cover it while I move to take position in this region to ensure we cover everything smoothly.'

We took on two former district champions in a do-or-die doubles match the following day. Sakshi's strategies worked to perfection—her understanding of the game ensured that we were always a step ahead in the mind games that seemed to be common at this professional level. What was expected to be a tough battle turned out to be an easy 21–10, 21–12 victory as we rode on our superlative form.

★ ★ ★

The remainder of the tournament turned out to be a mere formality for us. I won my singles finals with ease, and both of us lifted the doubles title in an emphatic fashion.

Celebrating our success, we found ourselves dining at Mainland China on the night of our doubles triumph, along with Purab and Adi.

As we settled in, Adi handed Sakshi a 'Congratulations' card. Her face lit up as she read it out and I gave him a thumbs up.

'*So smooth is your synchronization, so refined your rhythm, so unambiguous your understanding, so aggressive your attitude, so mellifluous your movement and so precise your placements—you girls are a blessing to badminton*' it read.

'Let's raise a toast, shall we?' Purab grinned.

We all raised our cups of lukewarm Chinese tea as our coach remarked, 'To the girls who make me love the sport even more, who are god's gift to the game and who make the future of Indian badminton sparkle—Payal and Sakshi!'

Over the course of dinner, he updated us on the road ahead.

'We will leave Pune in a couple of days. Mumbai is hosting the next level, the first state senior selection tournament. There will be three such tournaments in all, over the next three–four months. You will earn points according to your performance. At the end of it all, depending on your total points, your selection for the state team will be decided.'

My face lost a little bit of its shine.

'I thought we might get a break to allow us to go home,' I said, staring at the table.

'Well, the schedule is a little tight this time, can't help it. But after Mumbai, you will get a month's break before the second selection tournament.'

That cheered me up. I was dying to meet Bhaiya, Bhabhi and Mom. It seemed like ages since I had last seen them; so much had happened in the interim.

We got ready to move out in the next two days. I made a quick visit to Kavya's mausi's place to bid her a final goodbye.

'All the best, beta. It felt good when you girls were here. You brought so much colour and excitement to the house. We oldies don't really have much to do otherwise.' There was a tinge of sadness in her voice that made me sad too, as I hugged her. She had been so nice to us, looked after us so well.

'Pune felt like home only because of you, Aunty,' I told her. 'I promise I'll be back again to meet you. Thank you so much for everything.'

To my surprise, I also felt like cuddling Lyka. As I bent down to hold her paw and caress her back, I could see her eyes searching for Kavya. For the first time, I wished Lyka would feel the same way about me as well.

'You made me love dogs, Lyka. You are a darling. I'll never forget you.' I kissed her head.

Adi came with a bouquet of flowers, chocolates and a big 'All the Best' card to see us off at the bus stand.

'Don't forget me when you girls become superstars!' he joked.

I hugged him. 'You were the first person I played with, remember? In a way, this journey started with you, Adi. How can I forget you?'

As we climbed on to the bus, I looked back at him, the guilt in my eyes evident for him to read. He smiled back with a slight nod of the head.

'Maybe someday I *will* tell her, so don't worry,' he whispered.

As the wheels of the bus turned, so did the knob on my iPod. I resorted to the soothing beats of *Enigma* to calm my restless mind. Its echoes faded slowly into my subconscious. I drifted into a deep slumber as the bus rolled on smoothly, set to discover horizons far beyond my imagination.

12

City of dreams

There was something special about Mumbai that got me hooked—I couldn't place my finger on it, but it made me overlook the torturous local trains, the suffocating swarm of people, the interminable traffic jams, the irrepressible stench of fish and the cement and concrete all around. Was it the glittering ocean by the Gateway or the charming elegance of Marine Drive? Was it the extraordinary talent on display at the Oval maidan or the bustling energy at CST? Was it the funky clothing at Fashion Street or the unbelievable variety at Crawford Market? I wasn't sure. There was a buzz and spirit that kept the city alive and kicking.

Late one evening, a week into the training, I was busy practising, with Purab playing the role of the hard taskmaster to perfection. He stood on a large desk on the baseline of the court, racquet in hand, surrounded by shuttles all around him, while I occupied the other side of the court. From nearly eight feet above the ground, he fired shuttles one after the other to all parts of the court, mixing up his smashes and drop shots, to test my strength and agility. I was all over the court, stretching hard to reach out near the net and then running back to jump high to smash. Purab kept firing shuttles like a machine, and I soon started struggling to keep pace with him.

'You are slowing down, girl! Not covering the court well!'

I stopped to get back my breath.

'That's because you are killing me!'

'That is exactly what those girls are going to do to you in the tournament. I don't want any return from you to fall in the middle of the court; the four corners are your lifeline, remember that.'

I nodded and got ready to face the next barrage of shuttles.

As I hit the first one hard and got around quickly to cover my backhand, a big poster in the stands suddenly caught my eye:

'*Powerful Payal Packs a Punch!*'

It was the first time I had seen my name on a poster. I felt happy and confused at the same time. 'That's weird,' I said to myself. 'Maybe someone from Pune who saw my game is here as well.'

Two shots later, I plunged forward towards the net, but suddenly stopped short in my tracks. Held up near the old poster was another one, impactful enough for me to stare in astonishment.

It had a drawing of an engine running from the Imambada in Lucknow to the Gateway of India in Mumbai, followed by the words '*And the Payal Express Chugs On!*'

Too intrigued to continue now, I stood still on the court, staring at the posters, bewildered. Then I saw a figure appear from behind the poster and it seemed as if a current ran through my body. My racquet fell to the floor. I covered my wide open mouth with my hands, let out a shriek and began to cry.

In a flash, I ran off the court, jumped into the stands and hugged Bhaiya like never before! I wouldn't have let him go had I not felt a tap on my shoulder.

'So if the sob fest is over, am I permitted to intrude?'

The unmistakable mischief in the voice was enough to make me shriek a second time that evening.

'No way!' I exclaimed as I turned around, my face hot from the excitement.

'Look at you, Pihu; don't they give you something to eat here? Thank god we got kachoris for you from home,' was all Kavya managed to say before I literally jumped to hug her tightly as well.

Purab had climbed down from his desk and was watching the reunion with a smile.

'So . . . how, when, why, where?' I was at a loss for words.

'Well, it's simple, my dear.' Bhaiya laughed. 'This visit was long pending, but I was stuck with work. However, I finally managed to take a long break to see my little champion take the battle to those professionals!'

'How long are you guys going to be here?' I enquired, fearing the worst.

'Let's just say, long enough to see you win this tournament!'

My pitch suddenly hit a new high. 'Does that mean you will be here for Raksha Bandhan as well? Wait a minute; you planned it that way, didn't you?'

His smile was answer enough for me to hug him again. We had always been together on Rakhi every year and I would have been heartbroken had this year turned out otherwise.

However, my quest for clarifications was not yet over.

'How come you guys are here? I mean, how did you know when and where I will be?'

'Where there's a will, there's a way!' Kavya grinned, glancing at Sakshi, who had been standing quietly all this while, relishing the joy on her friend's face.

'You never cease to surprise me,' I smiled at Sakshi. 'I don't know how to thank you.'

'Move faster on the court during our doubles.' Sakshi laughed and winked.

'All right girls, why don't we all head back to Colaba now and catch up over dinner at home?' Bhaiya suggested.

'Oh, Mausi's place? She's back?'

'Yep! Just in time for us to pitch our tents there.'

Our mausi, who lived in Mumbai, had been out of town during the past month.

'Great! Can't wait to meet her after all these years! But . . . I am in the midst of my practice here . . .'

I looked at Purab with pleading eyes.

'Well, your coach has been very kind to give you an off this evening, as well as for some time every day next week. It's all been settled, dear sis,' Bhaiya smiled.

'As long as you don't disappoint me on the court!' Purab cautioned. I'm sure he was certain I wouldn't; he knew me well enough by now. In fact, I think he realized that this would only boost my confidence and relieve me of the pangs of loneliness that had been the only disturbing factor in an otherwise smooth training.

Kavya and I chatted endlessly in the taxi. We had so much to catch up on, even though we had regularly been in touch on the phone. That brief period of awkwardness had been wiped out from our lives and we were back to being best buddies, as if nothing had happened.

When we reached home, it was time for me to stare open-mouthed once again that evening.

'When the hell are you guys going to stop surprising me?' I exclaimed, as I hugged Vishakha Bhabhi joyfully.

'You deserve every one of these surprises, my dear,' Bhabhi replied with a smile in her usual soft tone, and patted me on the head.

That was a wonderful reunion night. I updated everyone with my experiences over the past few months, even though they had heard most of it over the phone already. Kavya was her usual chirpy and animated self, her big eyes dancing, her exaggerated expressions keeping us amused. Sakshi, though quieter, had mingled well with the group and seemed part of the family now. And Bhaiya and Bhabhi were happy enough to let us talk, while they smiled at each other and basked in the energy that engulfed the room.

The next week passed in a flash, while I practised as hard as ever under Purab's guidance.

Bhaiya told me that he had caught up with Purab one afternoon to talk about me.

'Do you really think she has it in her?' he had asked Purab bluntly.

'I will repent the most if I ruin your sister's career,' Purab had replied. 'Why do you think I am here with her, leaving all my work in Pune? The district team already has a coach, she doesn't really need me. Doesn't that speak for itself about the faith I have in her?'

'Are you satisfied with her preparations?' was Bhaiya's next question.

'Pretty much. As I always say, the only thing that can beat her is her own mind. As long as she thinks clearly and remains calm, she's good to go. My only concern is that she hasn't played any close three-setters where she had to dig deep, except for that one match against Sakshi. And at this level, all matches are expected to be close. I just hope she has the reserves to sustain the energy and momentum to play back-to-back tight games.'

I was touched to hear that Purab was so confident of my skills that he had left everything behind in Pune for me. I resolved to work harder than ever on my stamina and fitness.

On the eve of the first match of the tournament, I found myself sitting alone with Bhaiya on Marine Drive, gazing at the sunset, the splashing waves of the ocean soothing our anxious hearts.

'Stunning, isn't it?'

'Breathtaking! There is no urban location in the entire country more beautiful than this,' Bhaiya sighed, enamoured by the scintillating lights, the smooth, wide road, the cool breeze and the refreshing sound of the ocean.

We sat quietly for a while.

'Nervous?' he enquired, still gazing far out to the sea.

I continued to stare at the silhouette of the faraway ships, wondering what it would be like to be on one of them.

'A little bit,' I replied.

After a while, I was struck by a thought and asked Bhaiya, 'Do you remember how nervous I was at that poetry reading competition in class five?'

'How can I forget! You pulled me backstage and had they not stopped you, you might have dragged me on to the stage itself!' He chuckled slightly.

'And then that Shekhar came first—oh god, how much I hated him!'

Bhaiya smiled mischievously, 'Isn't he the same guy you were so jealous of? You once called me to your class and asked me to beat him up . . .'

'Oh come on! One must enjoy some privileges of having an elder brother in the same school! What good were you if I couldn't boss people around using your name?' I giggled.

Bhaiya laughed. 'But whenever you were called upon to perform anywhere, all your bossiness would fly out of the window! I remember all your annual sports days; you would be quivering with anxiety before the start of those races.'

'That too, after all your motivational speeches the previous night and your presence at the starting point. Had you not been there, I wouldn't even have been able to run!' I laughed.

'Had you spent more time focusing on the race rather than looking at me for inspiration, the walls at home would be boasting of golds instead of silvers!' Bhaiya teased.

I laughed, and then looked back at the ships, in deep thought.

'Now that I think about it, you have actually *always* been with me in all the important moments of my life . . . including now.'

Bhaiya didn't say anything. He just held my hand.

'What would I do without you, Bhaiya?' I looked at him and my eyes welled up.

He smiled at me. 'You'll thrash professionals on court, just as you did in the last tournament.' He wanted to keep it light; he knew it was imperative for me to relax before the big day.

I tried to smile, but couldn't. The affection in his eyes was enough to let me know how proud he was of me. I clutched his hands tighter, trying to convey my immense gratitude to him through my eyes.

We sat there for long, gazing silently at the sea, thinking back about the past years spent together.

It was the best conversation I had ever had with my brother.

13

A twist in the tale

It was a surprisingly dark and chilly morning the next day. I woke up early, not having slept well; the anxiety of the impending match was a tad too much for me. I knew I was in a far better frame of mind than in the last tournament, but there was something in the air that made me uneasy.

Sakshi was her usual cool self and got ready silently, lost in her own world. There was a glow on her face, a sign of how eager she was to take on the challenge.

On Bhabhi's strict orders, both of us, dressed immaculately in white with our kits on our shoulders, headed straight for the nearby temple before moving on to the stadium.

I don't know about the others, but a slight chill did run down my spine on reaching the venue and seeing a huge banner that read—'1ST MAHARASHTRA SENIOR STATE SELECTION TOURNAMENT'. It got worse from the moment I stepped inside the stadium, when people started turning towards me and whispering amongst themselves. I was clueless, but Purab remarked with a smile, 'Your Pune jersey is what's creating this buzz, my dear. Your name has been spreading fast on the state circuit; the girl who destroyed everyone in the Pune district selections! It's a small badminton world, Payal, and everyone is eager to see the player who has taken the stage by storm!'

I was confident all right, but there was still a weird uneasiness in my heart that I was finding hard to fight. It was not nervousness, it was not under-confidence, it was probably not even related to my game; however, like a sinister omen, it was haunting me.

'Let's do this, Payal. And don't forget what we discussed yesterday—she has a strong smash but weak court coverage; play patiently, make her run and she will start panting soon!'

As I stepped on to the court, a loud cheer arose from the stands. I looked up and smiled to see my vociferous family rooting for me. This was like a dream for them as well, and we were all relishing it to the hilt.

I was off the blocks in a flash—quite unlike me. Continuing from where I had left off in the last tournament, I hit hard, picked up the smashes with ease and made Vidya scamper around the court with my precise placements and deceiving drops. From the very first point, I made her reach out for the corners, taking full advantage of her sluggishness.

Bhabhi seemed completely astonished by my performance, and kept whispering to Bhaiya whenever I looked up at her between points.

Within no time, I raced to a 20–5 lead. The game had been completely one-sided so far. As I jumped high and thundered down a powerful smash from behind my head, not even giving Vidya seconds to reach it, the crowd started jumping and clapping.

Completely emotionless, I poured water on my face to cool down. Purab continued to whisper to me, but I wasn't listening to him. My uneasiness was still eating me up. I was sure it was not my game; I was playing well enough. Then why was I so restless? I tried hard to dig for an answer, but ended up feeling more frustrated, not being able to place my finger on it.

My shots became more tentative and my feet heavy as the second game progressed. I started committing unforced errors, and the sprint in my stride seemed to be deserting me. Vidya was quick to latch on to this momentary lapse of concentration and raised her game a notch higher, her smashes now raining with much more zeal and precision. It's funny how, at times, all it needs is a little spark to get the best out of a player. And Vidya was too experienced to let go of this opportunity. She unleashed an array of spectacular shots in successions, interspaced with brilliant deception on the backhand, to quickly build up a 15–6 lead.

I was now literally talking to myself to wake up from my slumber.

'What are you doing, girl? Come on now, pick yourself up. She's definitely not as good as you . . . make her move!'

But it was too little, too late for me. Vidya was on a roll now, having sensed blood, and was not going to let this one slip away.

'That's how professional sports is, I guess—you blink and you lose,' I mused, as Vidya completed a dramatic turnaround with a comprehensive 21–10 victory.

Standing next to the court with a towel in my hand, I saw that the colour had vanished from Bhabhi's face and she was holding Bhaiya's hand tight.

Purab was panicking a little as well, clearly evident from his gait. But his calm voice did wonders to my morale.

'No need to worry. She is still no match for you. Just remember, she tends to leave the backhand back corner open. Attack there incessantly, and you have got your game.'

I headed back to the court, murmuring to myself, 'Damn this uneasiness! I have worked hard to get here and I'm not going to let some silly, unknown fear ruin months of hard work!'

As the final game was about to start, a loud cheer shattered the nervous silence surrounding the court—'Go Pihu, go!' That was probably the loudest Kavya had ever shrieked, and I couldn't help but look up at her and smile.

Purab let out a sigh of relief as I hit the first service return hard down the backhand sideline, the spring back in my feet. I started attacking Vidya relentlessly on her backhand-back gallery, forcing her to scuttle diagonally across the court on almost every point. My focus was back on the four corners, as I punched out her trademark placements with panache.

But Vidya too rose up to the challenge in great style. She started to match me on every shot, and used her strong smashes deceptively, surprising me when I least expected them. She was much quicker on the court now and never let me run away with the lead.

We fought neck-to-neck until the score read 17–17. Things were tense now. There was a palpable nervous anticipation all around and no one dared utter even a word. My mind started playing games and somehow my restlessness returned at the worst possible time.

'Come on, Payal! You have come a long way . . . you can't throw this away now! Focus, girl, focus! Kiss the lines!' I was now talking aloud to myself, running out of breath, the intensity of the long game starting to take a toll on my body.

I didn't know what happened next, but by the time I pulled myself back, Vidya stood on three match points at 20–17. I had lost those points due to unforced errors I normally wouldn't have committed even during practice, and stood at the brink of being eliminated in the very first round!

I stood still and glanced around while Vidya walked up to the umpire to change the shuttle. Bhabhi was on the verge of tears. Kavya was pale and stared at the court incredulously. Purab simply stood near the court, unsure of whether to talk to me or leave me alone. And Bhaiya—well, he just looked at me intently, the same way he had on stage before my poetry recital in class five, the same way as on the track before I had sprinted off, the same way he had looked at me all my life, whenever I had felt unsure . . .

As I got ready to face the most important service in my career, he smiled and nodded his head. That was enough. I knew that he was always there for me.

I took a deep breath.

The serve was short. I returned deep, my hands sweating. Vidya smashed hard down the line. I leapt towards it and barely managed to return. She had gained control of the point, and made me scramble again . . . my mind was whirling, looking for an opening . . . I got my chance when I saw Vidya exposing the backhand gallery. I hit the shuttle hard there and followed it up with a well-timed smash down the forehand line.

Vidya was under pressure now. She tried to drop but I was too quick. I dropped it back . . . the shuttle kissed the net . . .

Bhabhi squeaked . . . Vidya still managed to return it, but I was on top of it in a flash. My final smash thundered towards the sideline. Vidya lunged . . . her racquet missed . . . the shuttle immaculately kissed the line and grazed to a halt.

A momentary silence, then loud applause roared across the stadium. I let out a sigh of relief.

I was back.

I won the next two points as quickly as I had lost the last three ones. Aggressive and accurate, I pulled together everything that I had and it was too much for Vidya.

Pumping my fists and letting out a loud cry of ecstasy, I was at my animated best as I saved three match points to take it down to the wire at 20–20. Bhabhi and Kavya had gone berserk now, standing on their feet, shouting my name.

I had got the momentum back and there was no way I was going to give Vidya another chance. Two more points after some breathtaking badminton and, within no time, I stood at the net shaking her hand, having bulldozed my way to a spectacular comeback!

Surrounded by everyone, as I stood near the court all drenched in sweat and trying frantically to win my breath back, I realized that I felt uneasy even after my spectacular victory.

'This is weird . . .' I said to myself, and just as I was about to give Bhaiya a hug, I suddenly stopped short. I looked up at him, worried.

'Where is Sakshi?' I asked.

'She left for her match sometime back. She's playing on Court No. 4. Why?'

I was off in a jiffy, and they followed me, confused.

'14–5,' I heard the chair umpire call out. I saw Sakshi serving, and breathed a sigh of relief.

'Is this the first game?' I asked a spectator.

'No, second. Sakshi won the first one 21–10.'

I instantly cheered up.

'21–10 and leading 14–5 . . . that's Sakshi the champ for you,' I gleefully pointed out to Bhaiya, much more relaxed now.

However, barely minutes after we had settled down in the stands to watch, something so unexpected and unfortunate happened that it shocked me to the core. Sakshi leaped high in her trademark style to smash down the line with all her strength and elegance. It was probably the most lethal shot she had ever hit, but as she returned to earth, she landed on her ankle, twisted her foot and fell down on the court with a loud cry, her pain and agony reverberating across the stadium.

For a few seconds the entire stadium was frozen by Sakshi's shriek. When we came back to our senses, we found her lying on the court writhing, unable to bear the excruciating pain, tears streaming down her cheeks.

The coach and physio rushed towards her and I followed them, on the verge of tears. I realized that my uneasiness had indeed turned out to be the ill-omen I had feared. Sakshi was unable to speak, and her right foot had started to swell. It was a no-brainer that she had to be immediately hospitalized. The next instant, Bhaiya and the physio took Sakshi to a nearby hospital that thankfully stood only five minutes away. Bhabhi, Kavya and I followed and by the time we reached the hospital, Sakshi was already inside the operating room, unconscious now from the stress and pain.

I sat stunned in the waiting room. Kavya sat beside me, holding my hand, whispering consoling words. It was an agonizingly long wait before the doctor finally called Bhaiya into his room. I followed too, and he knew it was useless to argue with me.

'I am afraid it doesn't look good,' said the doctor with a solemn face.

It was like a scene out of a movie.

He continued, 'Well, apparently her landing was quite bad. She has suffered multiple fractures, as well as a torn ligament on her right foot.'

I finally asked the question that had been haunting our minds for long now. 'How long before she can get back on court?'

'Very tough to tell; depends on her response to treatment and physiotherapy. It could be anywhere from four–five months to even a year.'

No one said anything for a while. My mind was whirling with emotions, driving me crazy.

'Does she know?' I asked.

'Oh yes, that's the first thing she asked after the operation, when I told her about the injury. She is under some sedatives now. You can meet her after an hour.'

'So, what next, Doctor?' Bhaiya enquired.

'Well, her leg will be in plaster for quite sometime, but she will be discharged in a couple of days. I will give you all the reports; she can go to any other doctor when she goes back home.'

My eyes were still moist as I left the room. We all sat outside, waiting for Sakshi to get up.

'Her dreams, her destiny, her desires—all gone down the drain in a flash,' I said slowly, looking out of the window, feeling emotionless now. 'Do you know, Bhaiya, that playing for India had been her dream all her life? This was what she lived for; this was her only passion in life. She spent all her school and college days sweating it out on court. This was the year she had been waiting for all her life; this was supposed to be her ticket to destiny!'

Bhaiya was quiet.

I sighed. 'It's not fair, Bhaiya . . . God is not fair.'

We all went inside Sakshi's room after a while and she looked surprisingly fresh, smiling at us.

'Thanks for getting me here.'

'Yeah, yeah, as if we would have left you crying on the court!' I smiled, trying hard to hide the pain in my eyes.

'I am sorry, Payal; I ruined your doubles chances!' she said, looking down.

I was angry now. 'Will you stop these sorrys and thank yous? I can't imagine how you can be so cool, smiling like this! I am dying inside, seeing my champ in plaster! And let the doubles go to hell . . . you are supposed to be out there on your own, like the queen of the court that you are!'

'But I'm not,' Sakshi replied impassively, trying hard to keep her eyes dry, her voice filled with regret.

Bhaiya tried to diffuse the tension in the room.

'Sakshi, I'm sure you will recover quickly and get back on the court sooner than you imagine. You have an athletic body that will respond very well to treatment—and it's not me saying this, these are the doctor's words.'

'Yes Bhaiya, I know.'

I was looking at her with astonishment. Sakshi was as unruffled as ever.

'I'll be back, Payal!' she said stoically. 'I have waited all my life for this dream, so what if I have to wait one more year?'

I hugged her tightly. She finally broke down as well. Bhabhi held my hand in a tight grip and Kavya went out of the room. She seemed genuinely sad for Sakshi, all the ill-feelings of the past forgotten now.

Amidst her sobs Sakshi quipped, 'Moreover, you still need a coach and psychologist; your mind can get screwed up even now.'

'You are officially hired,' I retorted, my sobs interspaced with laughter.

I was quite uneasy that evening as we left her to rest and went back home.

'It's all about destiny, Bhaiya, isn't it? You can fight and fight and fight . . . but you still can't change it.'

'Sometimes things are not in your hands, Payal, but that doesn't mean you should stop fighting.'

'What if my destiny has a similar story written?' I was slightly agitated now.

For a second I thought I caught his eyes flicker uncomfortably, but he recovered immediately.

'Calm down now, Payal. Don't be foolish. You can't lose faith.'

'It happened to the wrong girl! And I may be next . . .' I mumbled, putting on my shoes.

'Where on earth are you going?'

'For a run . . . Marine Drive.'

'You have a match tomorrow morning, and you played a long three-setter today. Are you crazy?'

'Does it matter? It's all destined in any case, isn't it?'

I ran hard that day, hard as I ever had. I was angry, I didn't know with whom, and this made me even more irritated. I felt restless and helpless at the same time, my heart trapped in the web of misfortune that had entangled Sakshi's life.

Slowly, my mind went blank, and all I could hear was the beautiful sound of the sea whispering in my ears. My shirt drenched in sweat and my lungs gasping for air, I kept on running as if under a spell, lost in my own world.

Finally I sat on a bench, facing the vast expanse of calm, blue water. I was breathing hard. Sweat dripped from my forehead on to my cheeks and mingled with a stream of tears, some angry, some sad. I sat there for a while, trying to make peace with myself, and then put on my iPod in a final attempt to soothe my mind as I started to trudge back. The soundtrack of *Chariots of Fire* seeped into my nerves and started to echo in the deepest corners of my heart.

When I reached home, I overheard Bhaiya talking on speaker phone to Purab.

'Don't worry, it's more important that she relaxes her mind. Her body will follow suit.' Purab's voice appeared calm.

'It's something else that I am worried about,' he continued.

'What?' Bhaiya asked.

'Her first match, despite the glorious fightback, was not supposed to go this way. This was only the first round and it should have been an easy game for her—things will only get tougher here on. I am not sure if she can continue with the same intensity, both mentally as well as physically, if all her future matches get so close. And on top of that, Sakshi's injury . . . I just hope all this doesn't mess with her head.'

I didn't feel like listening any further and left for my guest house. As I reached my room, I saw the empty bed near mine, lined by a racquet, a small idol and a photo of Sakshi's parents. I gazed at Sakshi's prized possessions for a while.

Something stirred inside . . . I smiled a little. I knew what I had to do. My destiny seemed clear.

14

The travesty of fate

For the next four days, I played the best badminton of my life. I was quicker, sharper and more powerful than I had ever been. With extreme focus and determination, I brushed aside the big names of the tournament to reach the finals in grand style, without even losing a game.

Sakshi, out of the hospital now with her leg plastered, played critic to prevent any over-confidence in me. 'You are getting predictable. Mix your short serves and long returns . . . you will remain a mystery that way.'

On the eve of my final match, a phone call came for Bhaiya. He went inside to talk.

I was in an intense discussion with Purab, whom we had invited home for dinner. He had got a video for me, just like during the coaching camp days, and we were dissecting the memorable 2007 Japan Open finals between titans Lee Chong Wei and Taufik Hidayat.

'Do you see how smart Lee is being here? Look at this point—Taufik was expecting him to attack down the line, but see how Lee slices the shuttle to find a cross-court fast drop!' Purab was pointing at the screen, playing the video in slow motion.

Bhaiya entered the room with a sullen face, dejection written all over it.

'I have to return to office tomorrow morning. Something urgent has come up,' he said slowly.

'What do you mean by tomorrow? You can't leave tomorrow!' I said, shocked.

'I know, Payal, I am sorry. I tried my best to explain to my boss and . . .'

'I don't care about your boss! You know that tomorrow is my final match, and on top of that, it's also Raksha Bandhan. How can you even think of leaving?'

'Yes dear, but I really can't help it. It's an emergency at office and I need to take the 10 a.m. flight.'

'Don't try to mollify me by all this "dear" sweet talk! After coming all the way, I can't believe that you are leaving before my finals. What happened to your "I will always be there for you" promise?'

Before anyone could say anything, I strode off to my room. I had never been so upset with Bhaiya! How could he even think of leaving before the biggest match of my career, the final match of the district tournament?

'That was quite rude of her,' I overheard Bhabhi say as I left. 'She should be mature enough to understand. She is behaving as if you are doing this on purpose.'

The next morning we all got ready quickly and assembled at the dining table. Rakhi had always been a grand affair at our home, and Bhaiya and I shared some wonderful memories of this day.

But I was not in my element, still angry with Bhaiya because he was not going to be with me in my final quest. I nonchalantly tied the rakhi on his wrist. The puja, too, seemed more a formality than anything else this time. Bhaiya, however, played his trump card, gifting me a small wrapped box.

Deep inside my heart, I wanted to rip that wrapping apart, fall in love with the gift and hug him with a big grin on my face. But I did not, to make it evident how angry I was with him. Not wanting to hurt Bhaiya's feelings beyond a point, though, I did open the box expressionlessly.

The box revealed a souvenir—an elegantly carved badminton court, with the lines and net made of silver, a gold-plated shuttle resting on top of the net and calligraphy etched on the front:

The lines of faith, the net of triumph,
Awe-inspiring has been your story
I pray to God these feathers of fortune
Forever guide you to glory

Everyone gasped at the gorgeous gift and raved about how beautiful it was. I, too, relented a bit on seeing it, held Bhaiya's hand lightly and smiled a little.

'Thanks so much,' was all I said.

As we all left home to board two cabs, one to take Bhaiya to the airport and the other to take the rest of us to the stadium, he hugged Bhabhi, bid the other two girls goodbye, and came up to me.

I stood motionless, looking straight at him, anger and disappointment written all over my face. But perhaps my eyes gave me away. Bhaiya looked at me with a knowing smile, and this time I gave a huge grin. Those few silent seconds were all the conversation we needed to be at peace with each other.

As I headed towards the stadium, I closed my eyes and said a silent prayer for him. I was sure he must have been doing the same for me.

Little did we know that god was listening to only one of us.

★ ★ ★

The stadium was jam-packed. My exploits had catapulted me to being referred to as a rising star, and I was no longer the underdog in the finals. My three-woman support camp settled just near the courtside, close enough for their cheers to reach me. Purab was already feeding me last-minute tips as I walked up and down after finishing my practice drill, sipping water.

Arpita, my opponent, was a veteran on the circuit. This was her third final in the last four years, but the title had always eluded her. She was determined to reverse her fortune this time and word was that this year was her best chance, playing against a debutante. Our match was so intense that I didn't even realize when forty minutes of the match had flown by. At the end of the second game, I found myself leaning against the railing on the courtside, panting hard and soaking in sweat, a towel covering my head. I had to keep wiping my face to stop the beads of perspiration that trickled uncontrollably on to my eyebrows. Meanwhile, I tried to focus on the diagrams Purab was drawing. I didn't want to discourage him, but I knew I was at a stage of the game where no theory would work; it was more a matter of courage and conviction.

A minute before I was to return to the court for the last time, I heard Bhabhi's voice somewhere close by, 'She fought bravely, winning the first game 21–19, but Arpita was too experienced for her in the end, and clinched the second game 21–17. They are taking a break now before the final game.'

The anxiety in her voice mirrored the mood in the stadium. I saw her approaching me, saying hesitantly over the phone, 'I don't know, she is in an intense discussion with Purab. I am not sure . . .'

I instantly waved at her and nodded my head. Purab didn't look pleased with the interruption but did not protest.

'Hold on, honey,' she whispered and handed me the phone.

'Didn't I tell you I will always be there with you in all your critical moments of life?' Bhaiya's voice was just the pick-me-up I needed then.

'I love you, Bhaiya,' I huffed, trying to catch my breath at the same time.

'So do I! How's the game going?'

'I feel it's under control. The very fact that I could beat her in the first game means I can surely do it again. And you know what? For the first time I feel that irrespective of whether I win or lose today, I know I truly belong to this stage.'

I paused, and then continued, 'And listen, I need to apologize. But I have to go now. Call me once you land.'

'May god be with you,' was all he managed to utter as I disconnected the call.

I stepped on to the court with a confident stride.

On the other side, Arpita stood firm with her head down, staring at the floor and listening patiently to her coach. She nodded receptively as her coach also drew his plans on paper.

I stared at them intently, experiencing a sense of déjà vu. Glancing up, I saw the huge floodlights shining on my face, the vociferous cheer piercing my ears. It suddenly occurred to me that I had been here before. I looked back at Arpita. As she stepped on the court for the final time, a loud roar reverberated across the hall. I felt that I had heard this roar before too, not recently, but long ago.

I stood rooted to the baseline, my mind perplexed. And then I thought I heard someone scream from the crowd, '*Come on, Ritu!*' But her name was Arpita . . . I didn't know if I was hallucinating, but by the time the game started, I felt like I was in a trance, oblivious to the commotion around me, trying to make sense of the bizarre tricks my mind was playing.

I tried to shake off the crazy thoughts and focus on the game. Both of us matched each other evenly at 15–15. It was then that my destiny started to change—for better or for worse, I couldn't tell.

15

From darkness to dawn

A few moments are all it takes to turn your world upside down.

Back in Lucknow the next day, my family and I stared mutely through swollen red eyes at the pyre. One part of me recalled my triumph at the court, while another simultaneously imagined what Bhaiya might have experienced on that sinister flight.

'Thud!' sounded my feet as I landed confidently on the wooden floor of the stadium. The smash I hit down Arpita's backhand proved to be deceptively quick for her to return. The crowd cheered loudly.

'Thud!' a loud noise suddenly erupted from the side of the aircraft, as it seemed to lose balance for a short while and swerved dangerously to the left. The passengers let out a cry of surprise.

Within minutes, Arpita's body started shaking with nervousness, as I was all over the court. Not only did I cover my four corners with ease, I threw her off-balance by making her scamper all across the court with clever variations and deceptions. Chaos reigned on Arpita's side now.

Within minutes, the plane started shaking wildly, and the overhead luggage compartments jolted open. Bags and suitcases tumbled out and flew all over the plane. Some people who were late in buckling up were thrown off-balance and scampered across the gallery, trying to hold on to the seats. Chaos reigned in the aircraft.

The stadium lights started fluctuating and we stopped our game for a while. I stood still, my head bent down, gasping for breath, my mind recalling memories that I had never seen before. I struggled to remain calm and forced my mind to relax amidst loud cheers from the stands.

The aircraft lights started fluctuating and the oxygen masks came down. Bhaiya pulled the mask over his face, gasping for oxygen as the air inside the plane thinned. He struggled to remain calm and forced his mind to relax amidst the cries of the other passengers.

Every time I descended after a thrilling smash, the crowd erupted with deafening applause, appreciating my play. I knew I was headed for my destiny and nothing could stop that. Happiness and calm was written all over my face.

Every time the plane descended further, the passengers erupted with deafening shrieks and cries, cursing their helplessness. Bhaiya knew he was headed for the end and nothing could stop that. Fear and panic was written all over his face.

My cross-court smash-landed with a loud thud, the shuttle skidding across the wooden floor before coming to a halt. I pumped my fists and cheered. But my cry got lost in the deafening roar of my supporters.

The plane crash-landed with a loud thud, and skidded through some woods before coming to a halt. Something hit Bhaiya hard and he cried out, but it got lost in the deafening roar of the other passengers.

My face covered with sweat, I took slightly unsteady steps across the court, too tired to run. All my steady shots kissed the sidelines, as I inched closer to victory.

His face covered with blood, Bhaiya took stumbling steps across the gallery, too injured to run. His wavering steps followed the glowing lines, as he inched closer to the emergency exit.

The stadium exploded with raging applause, as I stealthily dropped the shuttle cross-court very fine near the net, instead of hitting it high to the back gallery as expected. I now stood on the brink of victory.

The aircraft exploded into a raging fire, just as he had almost reached the exit, and he saw a huge ball of flame rush towards him, engulfing everything that came its way. He now stood on the brink of death.

I took a deep breath and closed my eyes. My life started flashing in front of me—the streets of Hazratganj in Kavya's company . . . the early morning chill at the Pune station . . . my quivering hands as I first held the racquet . . . training tirelessly in the gym for hours . . . Purab shouting 'kiss the lines' day after day . . . Sakshi's tears as she held her parents' photo and the pain in her eyes as she fell on the court . . . that ship far away in the ocean as I sat on Marine Drive holding Bhaiya's hand . . . And then I saw scenes that startled me. I saw myself lying on the court, watching the feathers glide by and land on the line . . . the stadium erupting, taking Ritu's name . . . Purab shaking his head in disbelief . . . blinding lights in my face as I sat in the car listening to Bhaiya's advice . . . And then I heard his voice again on the phone, 'May God be with you.' I opened my eyes. I felt lost.

Bhaiya took a deep breath and closed his eyes. His life started flashing in front of him—the thrill of that moment when he held a baby me in his arms, the nervousness in Bhabhi's eyes on the day of their marriage . . . the warmth of her touch as they took late night walks in the park near their home . . . the insecurity in his heart when I announced my departure . . . the rush in his blood as he saw me thrash a professional player . . . And then he heard my voice, 'I have found my destiny, Bhaiya.' He opened his eyes. He felt lonely.

With lightning speed I hit my final smash and dropped on the court with a cry, a tear rolling down my cheek. I closed my eyes in ecstasy, and opened them to the sight of clapping crowds.

With lightning speed the fire engulfed him, and within no time, he dropped on the floor with a cry. He closed his eyes in pain, never to open them again.

The mere thought of the cruel contrast sent a shiver down my spine as I continued to stare at the burning pyre.

I couldn't really put my finger on what was causing me more grief and anger—the fact that he had left the love of his life alone after having promised to hold her hand forever, that he had turned what could have been the happiest day of his sister's life into the worst one ever, or the fact that he had hastened the aging of his mother.

Kavya tried to keep everyone calm, though she herself was struggling to keep her tears in check. She never left Mom, Bhabhi and me alone, even for a second, and her presence prevented us from drowning in depression.

As the days went by, we gradually learnt to accept our fate and began picking up the pieces. One fine evening, Bhabhi and I stood on the terrace of our house under an orange sky, gazing at the setting sun, the breeze cooling our faces. She had moved in with us after the accident.

'I was so rude and harsh to him that day. I had never been so bitter to him before,' I recalled.

Tears were rolling down my cheeks. But I tried to maintain an impassive face and a steady voice.

'Life is too short for anger and hatred, Bhabhi, isn't it?' It was more of a remark than a question. 'I told him that I wanted to apologize to him after the match . . .' I broke off, and silence ensued. I had been filled with remorse ever since the news of Bhaiya's death.

The call for prayer from a nearby mosque reverberated across the neighbourhood.

'I will never forgive myself for the pain I caused him, when all he ever did was to love me and protect me.' My voice started to squeak.

Bhabhi hugged me tightly, not saying anything, as she wept uncontrollably.

We stood on the terrace till it became dark, Bhabhi having calmed me down by then. I was amazed by her strength and tenacity. She was probably the most distressed and forlorn of all of us, yet she was the pillar of support for everyone, never letting her feelings overwhelm her. Only sometimes I had heard her crying alone in her room, in the deepest hours of the night.

As we went into the drawing room, she asked me in a matter-of-fact manner, 'So, when are you starting your practice? The second state selection is only two weeks away, right?'

Mom, who had been knitting quietly in a corner, looked up at her and exclaimed, 'Are you crazy?'

'Why do you say that, Ma?' Bhabhi asked, taken aback.

'You know very well why!' Mom replied, tears rolling down her cheeks.

'But Ma . . .'

'Enough,' Mom ordered angrily. 'I have already lost enough, thanks to this evil game that has brought us nothing but bad luck. Payal will stay right here with me, and that's final. I don't want this topic ever discussed again in this house.'

Bhabhi went inside her room, fuming, and I decided to let her be for a while.

Later that night I knocked on her door.

'May I?'

'Of course, Payal, come in.' She was standing by the window.

I had decided to talk to her about something that had been troubling me. 'Bhabhi, will you be honest with me? I have been very confused for the past few days. Bhaiya's accident took my mind away from it, but now it is haunting me again.'

She looked at me enquiringly. 'What is it, Payal?'

I remained silent for a while. We could hear the leaves rustle outside in the night breeze.

'Where were we coming from when we met with an accident that night, four years back?' I finally asked.

I saw her stiffen a bit, but she kept a straight face. 'I wasn't married to your Bhaiya then,' she said, avoiding my eyes.

'I know,' I persisted. 'But Bhaiya would have surely told you the story.'

'What do you want to know, Payal?' She sounded tired.

'I want to know why I remember things that have never happened to me! Standing on the court that night against Arpita, I saw myself playing another match, Bhabhi . . . on some other court, against someone called Ritu! I have never played against any Ritu. And I know I was not hallucinating.'

Bhabhi turned back to look out of the window. I walked up to her and held her hand.

I whispered, 'I have a past which I don't know about, don't I?'

Bhabhi took a deep breath and closed her eyes. 'I don't know whether to be happy or sad that you've got your memory back.'

'I want you to tell me the truth, that's all. And I think I deserve to know it.'

'Payal, you were not supposed to know this. But what the heck! It was your brother who promised Ma, not me. And if it comes to this to save your badminton career, then so be it.'

She walked away from the window and sat down on the bed.

'Yes, what you saw was real . . . you used to be a star . . .'

And finally, after four long years, the secret of my life was laid bare. She told me all about my badminton past, the accident, the memory loss and Mom's decision to keep the game out of my life.

As she spoke, it all came back to me again, more clearly. It was as if I had never forgotten . . . just had a momentary lapse of concentration.

But what came next startled me to the core.

'It was your bhaiya's idea to send you to Pune.'

I was too stunned to speak. It was only after she shook me that I came back to my senses.

'So, you mean all this was part of a plan? The Pune trip, Adi's involvement, my visit to the stadium, Purab . . .? Did Kavya know? And Sakshi?'

'Kavya and Sakshi had no clue. But Adi and Purab had crucial roles to play to ensure that you got back on the court, which was once your life. You see, Bhaiya had already asked for Kuhu's mausi's help to get you to the court once you girls reached Pune, without telling Kuhu, of course. She did that with Adi's help and then Purab took over from there.'

I stared at her, incredulous. I remembered how Bhabhi had suggested Pune to Kavya in the first place, how Adi had invited me to play during the break that day, how Purab had selected me for the camp . . . the pieces were now slowly fitting together. I realized how the sport had always been in my blood. My old coach Purab had not changed a bit in four years, and he had been determined to get his old pupil back to where she belonged.

'But how did Mom agree this time around when I called to ask permission?'

'It was again your brother who fought for you and pleaded that you deserve a second chance.'

She looked away from me and continued, 'I think time had mellowed Ma down. She had rebuilt the family with great effort, and wanted things to remain simple and happy, as they were. It was not badminton that troubled her; she had just grown fearful of change.'

I was teary-eyed now. I had never understood how hard life had been for Mom.

'Ma finally gave in to Vaibhav's love for you, but only on the condition that you should never get to know of the past.'

'And which I technically got to know without you telling me,' I said, remembering all the scenes that had haunted me during my last match.

'It was a brave effort by your brother to give you back your dream,' Bhabhi said tearfully. 'For four years he lived with the guilt that he was responsible for the accident that took Dad away and ended your badminton career. Dad could never come back, hence his only aim was to somehow redeem your life.'

I was sobbing bitterly by now.

'Just before boarding the flight, he told me that his dream now was to read your name in the papers one day as a budding national player, and that he would pray to god every single day till that dream came true.

'His soul will forever remain ridden with guilt and will never find peace if he sees you sacrificing everything after having come so far. Nothing will hurt him more, Payal. It's rare for anyone to get a second chance. And he got you that.'

'I don't know what to do, Bhabhi,' I sobbed. 'I feel my career is jinxed. And how can I let Mom down? You know how broken she is.'

She came up to me and held my hand.

'We are all devastated, Payal, but we will make our peace with it.'

Taking a deep breath, she continued, 'I can't force you. It's your call. But do remember that though your brother could not live to see you reach the zenith of your career, it was his greatest desire. Do this at least for his soul now, as a mark of respect and gratitude for all that he had done for you all his life.'

Etching those words in my heart, Vishakha Bhabhi left the room.

My mind was numb. I had just got to know what my life had been, and I had no idea where it was headed. I knew she was right, but I didn't believe I had the courage and conviction to go back on court. I closed my eyes, trying to search for an answer, and before I knew it, I slipped into a deep slumber.

Well into the night, I had a familiar dream. I saw the same twin-seat fighter jet . . . the same cloud where I had played badminton with Purab . . . the same cheer from Bhaiya as he stopped the plane in mid-air to watch the game . . . the same laughter. And, just as before, I saw the plane lose balance and go into free fall, hurtling towards the ground.

I woke up with a start.

After a while, I went to the window and looked up at a star. I thought I saw Bhaiya's reflection there, and kept gazing at it for a while.

'I can't let you fall again, Bhaiya,' I muttered to myself.

16

A peaceful heart

I was jolted back to the present by Bhabhi shaking me.
'Are you okay? You did not respond at all to Kavya.'

I looked up at everyone in the room. Kavya was busy making funny faces at the newspaper, while Sakshi and Bhabhi were smiling at me. Mom was standing at the door, dabbing her moist eyes with her sari. This was my family; this was my world. Sitting with them, I felt a sudden sense of relief and security.

I cheered up.

'Kuhu, I am so sorry, but would you mind reading it again? After all it's not often that you see your name in the papers, is it?'

She winked at me gleefully. 'At your service, Your Highness!' Then she read out my interview again.

New Kid on the Court

In a land where only cricketers are revered, the emergence of a star in any other sport is a treat to savour. Particularly if it happens to be a girl.

She may not have reached there yet, but she sure is on her way. Meet Payal Malhotra, 18—the country's latest sensation, who has scorched the badminton circuit in the last eight months to storm into the national team in grand style. Oh and yes, before you ask what's the big deal, she was on the verge of becoming the junior national champion five years back when an accident supposedly ended her career. But like a phoenix, she has risen from the ashes to claim what she deserved for long. All this, after having suffered a huge personal tragedy late last year.

Lucknow News caught up with the new teenage star on the block:

LN: In a society where teenagers usually prepare for a lucrative career in medicine or engineering, how did you end up on a badminton court?

Payal: Destiny! I mean, I've loved the game since I was a kid, and my family has been supportive enough to allow me professional training. It was extremely tough juggling school with training. All I would do on a typical day was attend school, train at the stadium, eat and sleep . . . no time for anything else. And then I had an accident that changed everything . . . then I lost my brother, which again turned my life upside down. Well, life has been a roller coaster, but my passion for the game and my family's support has kept me going.

LN: How is it playing professional badminton at this level, especially after missing out on substantial juniors' experience?

Payal: Unbelievable! You think you know it all, having watched matches on TV for years, but once you are actually playing it, it's a whole different ball game. The first lesson I learnt was that half the game is won or lost not on the court, but in the gym. I saw how power and stamina can ultimately become the only dividing line between victory and defeat. I also realized how a nervous mind can so easily ruin a great talent. Calming my nerves has always been my biggest challenge, something that I have slowly learnt along the way, but not yet mastered.

LN: Who is behind the success you have tasted in such a short span of time?

Payal: Lots of people. My mom allowed me to get this far despite battling personal grief. My coach, Purab, turned me into a professional. My friend–cum–doubles partner, Sakshi, pulled me up whenever I was down. My sister-in-law got me back on the court when I had given up, and my best buddy Kavya stuck with me all along. But above all, it was my brother. I can talk all day about his contribution . . . but let's just say, I am what I am only because of him.

LN: Do you think it's tough for girls to succeed in sports, especially in a society like ours?

Payal: Yes, it is. But it's not just about guys or girls. Sports, in general, is an unconventional career in our country. If someone is a great player and also the class topper, you know what he or she will pursue, either by choice or by force. But again, you can't totally blame them. Money, infrastructure, stability . . . a lot of factors come into play. But I guess at the end of the day, if you are passionate and determined, the world is your oyster.

LN: How do you see the future of Indian badminton shaping up?

Payal: Gone are those days when it was an offbeat sport. We have now started to take the game more professionally, building it from the grass roots. There are champions waiting in the wings everywhere, and the circuit has never buzzed more. I hope we achieve enough international success for people to start widening their horizons beyond cricket.

And when I say champions are waiting, I mean it literally. I know one potential champion personally. You would have probably been taking her interview today instead of mine, had fate not interrupted her plans this year. But watch out for her next season . . .

LN: So, what's next for you?

Payal: Well, I am headed for the national training camp in Delhi next week, from where we'll directly go to Beijing. It's going to be my first international tournament, and the beginning of a new life for me. So yeah, you can say I am excited!

LN: From us and our readers, all the best, Payal, and hope that you bring laurels to the country!

Kavya put the paper down and announced with a mischievous grin, 'My name is in the papers, ladies . . . in the papers! This goes into my bio-data!'

She bowed to me in style, then gave me a warm hug. Just then her mobile rang. She smiled on seeing the screen and picked up the call.

'Hey Adi . . . yeah, of course we saw it. In fact, we were all reading it together right now.' She winked at me in her typical mischievous

way and started strolling out of the room, the phone still stuck to her ear. 'Make a trip to Lucknow over the upcoming long weekend na . . .' I could hear her tone mellowing. Adi and Kavya's friendship had only grown stronger over the last year, and I was in no doubt that the next level in their relationship was not far away.

Sakshi was sitting in a corner. Initially, her face had lost its colour, probably at the thought that the article would have been about her, had she not been so unfortunate. But by the time the narration was over, she was beaming. She held my hand and smiled.

I smiled back. 'I'll be waiting for my doubles partner . . . just watch where you land next time.'

Sakshi giggled.

As I got up to go to my room, Bhabhi came up to me and handed me a beautifully framed newspaper cutting, the wooden borders boasting of exquisite artwork—it was the same article! Engraved on the frame below the article were the words, 'Thanks for fulfilling my dream. May this be just the beginning . . . Always with you—Bhaiya.'

Neither of us said a word. We just hugged each other, our moist eyes saying it all.

I came back to my room and closed the door. It felt peaceful being alone. Slowly, I walked to the shelf and placed the frame neatly on it. My eyes shifted to the silver badminton court souvenir resting nearby, and I gazed at it for long, moving my fingers lightly over the inscription.

*'I pray to God these feathers of fortune
Forever guide you to glory'*

A roar of thundering Sukhois shattered the silence of the skies. Tiny tears glistened in my eyes.